Charles Morris

Tales from the Dramatists

Vol. 2

Charles Morris

Tales from the Dramatists
Vol. 2

ISBN/EAN: 9783337376130

Printed in Europe, USA, Canada, Australia, Japan

Cover: Foto ©Andreas Hilbeck / pixelio.de

More available books at **www.hansebooks.com**

TALES FROM THE DRAMATISTS

BY

CHARLES MORRIS

IN FOUR VOLUMES

VOLUME II

WITH PORTRAITS

PHILADELPHIA

J. B. LIPPINCOTT COMPANY

1893

PRINTED BY J. B. LIPPINCOTT COMPANY, PHILADELPHIA.

CONTENTS.

LIST OF ILLUSTRATIONS.

VOLUME II.

THE GAMESTER.

BY EDWARD MOORE.

[THE author of the thrilling domestic tragedy of "The Gamester," one of the strongest lessons against the evils of gambling ever presented, was born in 1712, the son of a dissenting minister of Abingdon. The play is lacking in literary merit, but is constructed with much dramatic skill, and the career of Beverly, the gambler, affords excellent opportunities for stage effect. Moore also wrote two comedies, and an imitation of Gay's fables that became very popular. He died in 1757.]

In London, about two centuries ago, there lived a gentleman named Beverly, who was possessed with such a passion for gaming that he had, through his devotion to cards and dice, wasted an ample fortune, and brought himself to the verge of ruin. This unfortunate state of affairs was largely due to his unbounded trust in a seeming friend named Stukely, who, while pretending commiseration for the family, and a desire to reclaim the gambler, had contrived to rob him of his estate by surrounding him with a set of sharpers, his tools and confederates. The wealth which Beverly had lost had gone mainly into the pockets of this supposed friend, through the aid of false dice and fraudulent play. Stukely had other ends in view than the ruin of his blinded dupe. Mrs. Beverly's beauty had attracted his licentious eyes, and the overthrow of her virtue was one of the main objects in his nefarious schemes.

As for this lady, her husband's ruinous passion for gambling had reduced her to the utmost distress. She had beheld his own fortune, and the one which she had brought him, vanish before her eyes, until now her house and furniture had been sold to pay the accumulating debts, and she, with Charlotte, Mr. Beverly's sister, had retired to humble lodgings, whither they were pursued by creditors. Of her once abundant means Mrs. Beverly had only her jewels left. Charlotte's fortune was also in her brother's hands; and there was reason to fear that now, having dissipated his own and his wife's estates, he might squander hers or the wretches who had robbed him of his own.

There is still another person of whom we must speak, Mr. Lewson, a devoted lover of Charlotte, and a generous friend, who had secretly bought in the Beverly house and furniture, which he held for the use of the unhappy wife. His courtship of Charlotte had so far proved unsuccessful, her sympathy for her suffering sister-in-law being so great that she would not listen to anything that might part them. As for her fortune, which Beverly falsely assured her was still untouched, she determined to remove it from his hands, if possible, and use it for the support of the gamester's reduced family.

On the occasion when we first meet these unfortunate women, Beverly had been absent all night, and his poor wife was in a state of the deepest sorrow and apprehension, for he had never before left her alone for a night. While Charlotte was seeking to comfort her, they were visited by an old servant of the family named Jarvis, a faithful old man, who greeted them with so much feeling as to bring tears to Mrs. Beverly's eyes. He begged to be permitted to attend Mr. Beverly at his own expense, and seek to withdraw him from his evil ways.

Mr. Stukely called immediately afterwards, with words and tones of the deepest sympathy. He expressed surprise and alarm that Beverly had not returned, declared that he had lavished good advice on him without effect, and had supplied him with money to the injury of his own fortune. Where he was now he could not tell. He had left him, he said, the evening before at a place called Wilson's, in company he did not like. If Mr. Jarvis wished to find him, he might seek him there.

Jarvis left for this purpose, and a knocking at the door calling Charlotte from the room, Stukely was left alone with Mrs. Beverly. He took instant advantage of the opportunity to further the base scheme that nestled in his brain, insidiously hinting to the unhappy wife doubts of the cause of her husband's absence, and striving to arouse jealous feelings in her mind.

"Yet the world is full of slander," he said. "If you are wise, you will turn a deaf ear to such reports. 'Tis ruin to believe them."

"Why name them, then?"

"To guard you against the voice of rumor. These tales may reach your ears from other tongues."

"What tales? By whom? Who doubts my husband's faith? You are his friend,—and mine too, I trust. Only for that I had been unconcerned."

"For Heaven's sake, madam, be so! I meant to guard you against suspicion, not to arouse it."

"Nor have you, sir. I have a heart suspicion cannot reach."

"Then I am happy. I pray you, let this go no further. I would say more, but am prevented."

His insidious hints were brought to an end by the return of Charlotte, who said that a creditor had called, but had been dismissed by Jarvis. Immediately afterwards Mrs. Beverly left the room, in a dispirited mood, saying that she was faint with watching and must take some rest.

Stukely watched her with cunning eyes, well knowing that it was the poison he had breathed into her ear that affected her spirits. He had played the first card in his evil game. While he stood conversing with Charlotte, Mr. Lewson entered, and asked for Mr. Beverly. On learning of his continued absence, he turned to Stukely with a hostile expression of countenance.

"I inquired for you at your lodgings, sir," he remarked.

"For what purpose, pray?" asked Stukely.

"Only to congratulate you on your late successes at play. Poor Beverly! But he should take some comfort in having such *successful* friends."

"What am I to understand by this?" demanded Stukely, angrily.

"That Beverly is a poor man, with a rich friend. That's all."

"Sir, this needs an explanation. Another time I shall demand one."

"Why not now? I am no dealer in long sentences. A minute or two will do for me."

Stukely, however, whose courage ran far short of his villany, was just then not anxious for an explanation; and sheltering himself behind the excuse of a lady's presence, he took his leave, declaring that he was ready to hear from the gentleman at any future time.

"What mean you by this?" demanded Charlotte, in a tone of surprise.

"To hint to him that I know him."

"Know him? This is mere doubt and supposition."

"I shall have proof soon."

"And would you risk your life——"

"My life? With Stukely? Have no concern, Charlotte. I know the fellow well. It would be as easy to make him honest as brave. But I hear Mrs. Beverly coming. Let this be a secret between us. She has already too much to trouble her."

Stukely, meanwhile, betook himself to his lodgings, where he soliloquized over his projects. He had loved Mrs. Beverly before her marriage, and now thirsted for revenge on the man who had robbed him of her, and whom he sought to repay by robbing him of his wealth. There still remained to Beverly his wife's jewels and the reversion of his uncle's estate. These Stukely declared to himself he must have, to complete the gamester's ruin. Beverly must demand his wife's jewels. Once in the tempter's hands, he could use them to add fuel to her jealousy.

His soliloquy was interrupted by the entrance of one of his chief agents, a fellow named Bates.

"Our forces are in readiness," he said, "and only wait for orders. Where is Beverly?"

"At last night's rendezvous. Is Dawson with you?"

"Yes. Dressed like a nobleman; with money in his pocket, and a set of dice that would deceive the devil."

"That fellow has a head to undo a nation. But for the rest, they are such low-mannered, ill-looking dogs, I wonder Beverly has not suspected them."

"That matters nothing, if they have money.

The passion of gambling casts such a mist before the eyes, that the nobleman may be surrounded with sharpers, and yet imagine himself in the best company."

And so they went on, laying their plans, not the least of which was a resolution to *take care* of the suspicious Lewson, whom Stukely declared would ruin them if they did not checkmate his designs.

While these events, caused by and revolving round Beverly's insane infatuation, were taking place, that person was seated in the gaming house which had been the scene of his chief losses. His soul was filled with remorse, which was added to by the entrance of Jarvis, who deeply impressed upon him the sad state in which he had found his wife. But the beneficial effect which these admonitions might have had was prevented by the entrance of his evil genius, Stukely, who laughed at the misgivings of his dupe and bade him cheer up, telling him that fortune must soon turn in his favor. As for himself, he declared that he was ruined also, and even in danger of prison for his debts, but that he was not the man to give up hope. "Have you nothing," he asked; "no movables, no trinkets, that can be converted into money? Your wife's jewels?"

"And shall this thriftless hand seize them, too?" exclaimed Beverly, in deep distress. "My poor, poor wife! Must she lose all? I could not wound her so."

"No matter. Let it pass. What if a prison be the reward of friendship? It is what one must look for."

"Leave you to a prison! No; fallen as you see me, I am not such a wretch as that! My wife's jewels?—But in friendship's cause?—I'll do it!"

Beverly left the house in a passion of feeling for his friend, and returned home, resolved to make any sacrifice to save him from prison. His wife met him with a love that ignored her wrongs. So kind was her greeting, indeed, that the remorseful gamester had not the courage to hint at the purpose which had brought him. But this possibility Stukely had foreseen and provided for. He sent a letter after his dupe, which reached him while in conversation with his wife. In this he declared that he had determined to trespass no further on his friend's bounty, but would leave England and thus escape the danger that threatened him, rather than resort to the means they had talked of.

The blinded dupe read the letter to his wife, who earnestly insisted on knowing what means these were, and on learning that the writer alluded to her jewels, she begged her husband to take them.

"What are these trifles, if weighed against a husband's peace?" she declared. "Let them pur-chase that, and the world's wealth is valueless beside it."

The ruined gamester, however, did not fare so well with the other inmates of his house. Lewson spoke so plainly of his doubts of Stukely that a quarrel nearly arose between them; while Charlotte pressed him so closely in regard to her fortune that he was put to straits to hide the fact that it had sunk into the same gulf which had swallowed his own, and only escaped her questions by promising to satisfy her in the morning.

The result of this last venture with the goddess Fortune was but what might have been expected. The jewels were converted into money, the money pressed upon Stukely, and at the gaming table it quickly went where so much had gone before it, into the hands of the gang of soulless sharpers.

The reverse, from a venture which Stukely had made to appear so promising, almost overturned Beverly's reason. He turned fiercely on his false friend, accusing him of being the demon who had first induced him to gamble, and led him on from loss to loss by his insidious counsels; and was only prevented from assailing him by his earnest protest that he too had been ruined.

Beverly's passion, thus diverted, next turned against the sharpers who had ruined him, and whom he now declared must have done so by fraud.

"Yet the world speaks fairly of them," said Stukely. "We have watched them closely, too.

But it is a right usurped by losers to think the winners knaves. Let us have more manhood, Beverly."

"I know not what to think," cried Beverly, in despair. "This night has stung me to the quick; blasted my reputation, too. I have bound my honor to these vipers; played meanly on credit, and have no means to pay."

Stukely insidiously hinted, in reply, that one means of redress remained, which would enable him to pay his debts and would yield him a sum to retrieve his losses. This was, to sell the reversion to his uncle's estate. Bates was wealthy and would purchase it.

"Be it so," exclaimed the desperate gamester. "Succeed what will, to-night I'll dare the worst. 'Tis loss of fear to be completely cursed."

Stukely, congratulating himself on having led his dupe so far on the road to ruin, now proceeded to put into effect the scheme directed against the honor of his wife. Leaving Beverly to visit Bates, and add his prospects of future fortune to the sum of his previous losses, the villain sought the humble abode which now formed the unfortunate lady's home.

On meeting her, he declared that he had parted from Beverly that morning in anger, and on her speaking of the letter which had induced her to yield up her jewels, he stated, with a pretence of indignation, that it was a false one, a mean contrivance to rob her of the little that remained to her. He vowed that it had not been written by him, but by Beverly himself, and that the jewels yielded him by his wife had been lavished on a wanton.

This well-devised plot, which he unfolded with the greatest show of feeling, declaring that he spoke from personal knowledge, convinced the trusting wife that she had been cruelly deceived; and in the fire of her resentment, she declared that she would be revenged on him who had so deeply injured her.

"Redress is in your power," he said.

"What redress?"

"The marriage vow, once violated, is in the sight of Heaven dissolved. Start not, but hear me. You owe no loyalty to him who has injured you so deeply. Fly from the cruelest of men for shelter with the kindest; from him who wrongs you to him who dares tell you that he loves you."

During these words Mrs. Beverly had gazed upon the speaker with startled eyes, amazement gradually turning to indignation as he went on. When, in the end, he fully revealed his base duplicity, she broke out with a fury that could no longer be restrained.

"Would that these eyes had heaven's own lightning, that with a look I might blast you!" she exclaimed. "Am I, then, fallen so low? Has poverty so humbled me that I could listen to a hellish offer, and sell my soul for bread? O villain! villain! But I know you now, and thank you for the knowledge."

Stukely listened with startled ears to this un-looked-for reception of his base proposal. He had played and failed. Nothing remained but to seek to hide his baseness, and he endeavored to do this by threats.

"I scorn you and your threats!" she indig-nantly replied. "Beverly shall know of your base proposal, and revenge me on his false friend."

"Be it so. Send him for defiance, if you will. I'll make a widow of you, and then can court you honorably."

"O coward! coward! your soul will shrink before him! And yet——" She hesitated. "Be-gone; keep your own secret. Leave me, despi-cable wretch!"

The exhausted woman sank feebly into a chair, as the discomfited villain left the room with renewed threats. What to do she knew not. Should she speak, and perhaps doom her husband to death? Should she be silent, and leave him still exposed to this villain's temptations? Her soul was torn with doubt and agony. That Lewson was right in his suspicion of this man she now plainly perceived. He, and he only, was the ser-pent who had lured her weak husband to ruin.

We have dwelt so long with the guilty and the miserable personages of our story that it will be a relief to turn to two on whom happiness had fallen. In the midst of these distressing events, Lewson had taken the opportunity to press his suit again upon Charlotte, and this time with success, she having yielded to the warm demand which she had long repelled, and promised to be his wife, whatever might occur. Armed with this assurance, he now told her what he had hitherto concealed. He had learned from Bates, Stukely's chief agent, that her fortune was lost. It had followed Beverly's own estate into the yawning gulf of ruin.

"Bates is grateful to me for a service I have done him," he continued. "He told me this in friendship, thinking to warn me against you, and little deeming that his news would give me new courage to seek to win you."

"It was honest in him, and I thank him for it."

"I hope to learn more from him," added Lewson. "He is deep in Stukely's confidence."

The joy of the newly-betrothed pair received a shock when they met Mrs. Beverly, for the unhappy woman, still burning with indignation, had resolved to disdain Stukely's threats, and told them of the insult she had received from the soulless villain.

"The smooth-tongued hypocrite!" exclaimed Charlotte, in fiery indignation.

"We have found him out,—that is something gained," declared Lewson. "For his insults I promise you retribution."

"No violence!" broke in Mrs. Beverly. "I only spoke on your promise."

"Trust me to be cool and quiet. Yet I'll charge him strongly, and draw my conclusions from his looks and answers.   Next I'll seek Bates and sift him to the bottom.   If I fail there, some of the gang can be bribed to betray the others.   Good-night; I'll save your husband yet.   But no time is to be lost."

Leaving the house, Lewson proceeded without delay to Stukely's residence.   A hot and violent conference ensued, in which the visitor accused his villanous host of guilt and treachery in a tone that threw him into trembling confusion.

"You sheltered yourself, when we last met, behind a lady's presence," cried Lewson, in a hot passion.   "Now we are alone.   Why, what a wretch!" he continued, as Stukely cowered before him.   "The vilest insect will turn when trampled on; and this thing calls itself a man!"   He flung his craven antagonist fiercely from him.   "Villain, if you would save yourself, fall to confession.   If not, I'll crush you like a worm."

This Stukely, roused by the very extremity of his danger, refused to do, though Lewson drew his sword and threatened him with death unless he made a full revelation of his villany.

"He *is* within my grip," exclaimed the wretch, stung at length to bold defiance.   "Do not push me too far, or the hand that has supported him shall fall and crush him."

"Why, now there's spirit in you!   Do your worst, villain, I'll reach you yet.   Beverly shall be saved, you cur, and you punished; take my word for that. You shall hear from me again," and Lewson left the room in a high passion.

"Curse on my coward heart!" exclaimed Stukely. "I'm shaking like a leaf at that fellow's vaporing. But he must be dealt with; the officious fool will make mischief else."

His method of dealing with him was one in consonance with his cowardly and ruthless nature. On the entrance of Bates, shortly afterwards, Stukely told him of Lewson's visit and threats, and coolly proposed that he should be despatched by the assassin's blade, as the safest method of ridding themselves of a dangerous foe.

Bates started at this proposition, and at first refused to have anything to do with it. But on Stukely's declaring that they must crush Lewson or he would crush them, that shame and beggary would be their lot were their villany once exposed, and that he would share his gains with him who struck the blow, his confederate withdrew his refusal.

"How shall it be done?" he asked.

"He's gone to Beverly's. Wait for him in the street. The night is dark and fit for mischief."

"Consider it done, then," said Bates, as he left the room. "Farewell till it is accomplished."

"Why, farewell Lewson, then, and my fears with him," soliloquized Stukely. "This night secures me. I'll wait the event within."

Meanwhile the ruin of Beverly had been completed. He had sold the reversion of his uncle's estate to Bates, staked the money at the gaming table, and again lost. The result was crushing. In the words of the leader of the gang: "When all was lost, he fixed his eyes upon the ground, and stood some time, with folded arms, stupid and motionless. Then, snatching his sword, which hung against the wainscot, he sat down, and, with a look of fixed attention, drew figures on the floor. At last he started up, looked wild and trembled; and, like a woman, laughed out aloud, while tears trickled down his face. Thus he left the room."

The frenzy of the ruined gamester, indeed, was almost madness. He roamed the deserted streets like a lost spirit, now mourning with remorse, now breaking into rage at his folly, now weeping like a child. In this mood he met Lewson, and turned on him with anger, declaring that he had traduced him, and spread a vile report that he had wronged his sister.

Drawing his sword, Beverly advanced in a hostile manner, calling sternly on his late friend to draw and defend himself. This Lewson refused to do, and declared that this accusation was a falsehood, of which Stukely was the inventor.

"As you please; it *was* Stukely that accused you," said Beverly.

"The lying dog! He fears discovery, and would have you kill me to screen himself."

"Can you prove this?"

"Yes; give me till to-morrow, and I will."

What further took place in that scene of midnight gloom and human passions a few words will tell. Bates, who was abroad on his murderous mission, had overheard the quarrel between Beverly and Lewson. As he stood viewing them from a distance Jarvis appeared.

"Yonder's your master," he said to Jarvis. "Go to him, and lead him home. I prefer not to be seen by him."

He withdrew in the direction Lewson had taken, leaving to the heart-broken old servant the sad task of quieting his frenzied master, and persuading him to return home.

The subsequent events may be fitly told in the words of Dawson, the leader of the gang of sharpers, who had been in company with Bates when the quarrel between Beverly and Lewson took place, and hastened with news of it to their employer.

"Why, this is excellent!" exclaimed Stukely. "That quarrel fits neatly into my plans. Bates will do it, think you?"

"He shrunk from it at first; but when we parted, it was decided between us that Lewson should die."

"Good! Beverly killed him; remember that. A jury shall so decree it, after hearing your testimony about the quarrel. Here, take this writ; I have had it by me for some days, awaiting a convenient time for its execution. It is for money that I have loaned Beverly.

Find an officer and have him arrested instantly."

"Arrest a beggar? He cannot pay you."

"Dull fellow, can you not understand? Beverly was seen quarrelling with Lewson; I, who know his intentions, had him arrested as a friend, to save him from murder. I was too late, as it will appear, but my act was well meant, and men will thank me for it. Now do you understand?"

"Perfectly."

"Then to work, wait about his door, and have him seized when he comes home. A jail must be his lodging this night."

All was, or seemed to be, carried out in accordance with Stukely's orders. An hour afterwards Dawson returned, and told a moving story of the arrest of Beverly at his own door, and the anguish it had caused his wife and sister. Even *his* hard heart had been moved thereby, and had the officers been as compassionate as he the arrest would not have been made.

"He is safe in prison, then?"

"Yes; with only Jarvis to comfort him."

"There let him lie till we have further business with him. And for you, let me hear no more of compassion. A fellow nursed in villany has naught to do with such womanly weakness."

"Say you so, sir! You should have named the villain that tempted me."

"'Tis false. I found you a villain, and so employed you. But no more of this. Ah! here comes Bates. Now, Dawson, for medicine to strengthen your weak heart."

The story that Bates had to tell, indeed, was a horrible one. Lewson was dead,—stabbed to the heart. Their pathway was clear so far as this enemy was concerned. Stukely listened to the details of the murder without a shudder, and eagerly set to work to complete his plans to lay the crime on Beverly.

" Jarvis saw the quarrel too, you say?"

" Yes; or heard it at a distance."

" Good; unwilling evidence carries weight; he shall be forced to speak."

Had the soulless wretch heard the words that passed between his villanous tools after they left him, his self-congratulation would have been greatly reduced.

" Your story, then, is all imaginary?" asked Dawson.

" Every word of it. I draw the line at murder. But Lewson will keep out of sight till the proper time. A cursed wretch that Stukely."

" Why, hang it, he has gone too far! To seek to hunt his dupe to the death! I'm with you, Bates. But are you safe?"

" Yes. Lewson is with us."

Beverly, as Dawson reported, had been conducted to a debtor's prison, where he passed a wretched night, despite all Jarvis's efforts at consolation. Tears, sighs, remorseful self-accusings, wild outbreaks of despair, made the old man as miserable as his unhappy master, and morning dawned before the faithful attendant succeeded in bringing the ruined gamester into a calmer mood. In the end he appeared to become composed and easy, and strongly insisted that Jarvis should return to his home, and do what he could to comfort his wretched wife.

The miserable and desperate man had a secret purpose in this of which his old attendant did not dream. In the despair of the past few days he had provided himself with poison, and no sooner had Jarvis left the cell than he took the fatal vial from his pocket, and sat long with his eyes fixed gloomily upon it, while dark thoughts passed through his mind.

"Why, there's an end, then," he said, at length, in hollow tones. "I have judged myself fully, and the verdict is *death*. The load of life oppresses me too much, and my soul's horrors are more than I can bear. Conscience, thy clamors are too loud. Here's that shall silence them." He gazed fixedly at the vial. "Come, then, thou cordial for sick minds. Let this be my last throw in life. Will it be a losing one, like all that have gone before? Who shall say?" He drank from the vial, and threw it from him. "Now, death is in my veins. But let it come. I have lived too long."

Too long, indeed, for he had lived long enough to lose at the gaming table a second fortune, greater than his own. Unknown to him, the uncle, the reversion of whose estate he had sold, was now dead, and had willed him his entire property. This important news Jarvis learned while on his way to Mrs. Beverly's lodgings, and he broke in upon the afflicted women with a tale of joy that lifted them from despair to ardent hope. The uncle had died on the previous day, and Beverly was rich again. They must fly to his prison-cell, and bear him the good news. He was now quiet and calm: the tidings would lift him from despair to joy.

Having hastily told this story, Jarvis hurried out for a coach, and in very few minutes the two women were flying to the prison, eager to release the unhappy captive. Little did they dream of the fatal act which he was even then performing.

To their surprise, the news was received by Beverly in a manner the reverse of joyful. He heard his wife and sister to the end, questioned them in a strange manner, that excited their apprehensions, and then broke out with fierce self-upbraidings.

"Wretch that I am!" he cried. "All this large fortune, which might have made us happy, has gone before it came. In a cursed hour, I sold all my claim to it last night."

"Sold it?"

"Yes. That devil Stukely tempted me to the deed. I sold the reversion to pay false debts of honor, and—lost the money among villains."

"Then, farewell all!" cried Charlotte.

"Liberty and life!" groaned the miserable gamester. "Curse me, for I deserve it."

He was answered by his faithful wife in a manner he had no reason to expect. Kneeling at his feet, she prayed to Heaven to save him from despair, and vowed that she would toil for his support while she had hands to work with.

"It is too late!" he cried. "I have done a deed that cannot be retrieved; a deed that seals your misery here and mine hereafter."

"A deed? What deed? Surely he raves, Charlotte. Yet his looks terrify me."

"I fear the worst," said Charlotte, with apprehensive countenance. "What is it, brother?"

"A deed of horror.—Ha! villain, what brings you here?" His eyes were fixed fiercely on Stukely, who entered at that instant.

"I came to bring you safety. The arrest last night was well meant, but came too late. Here, madam, is his discharge." He handed Mrs. Beverly a paper. "Let him fly instantly."

"Fly!—from what?" cried Charlotte.

"I would have kept his hands from blood, but was too late."

"From blood! whose blood? Is this the deed he spoke of? Whose blood, villian?"

"From Lewson's blood."

"Lewson!" cried Charlotte, rushing, white with terror, towards him. "We have not seen him to-day. What of him? Quick!"

"He is dead. Murdered, men say."

"Murdered! Lewson! Oh, horrible! Who has killed him?—Brother, he charges you——"

"Silence all," exclaimed Beverly. "Proceed, sir. What have you more to say?"

"Nothing," answered Stukely. "Here comes the evidence of my words." Bates had entered while he spoke.

"Take comfort, madam," said Bates to Charlotte. "There's one without asking for you. Go to him at once."

"Oh, miserable me! Lewson slain! My brother!" faltered Charlotte, with a face of deathly pallor, as with trembling steps she complied with Bates's request.

"Follow her, Jarvis," exclaimed Mrs. Beverly. "Her grief may kill her."

"Jarvis must stay here," replied Bates. "He is needed, madam."

"Rather let him fly," said Stukely. "His evidence may crush his master."

"Why, what means all this?" asked Beverly. "What new villany—— Oh, I am sick! Bring me a chair!"

As Mrs. Beverly hastened to help him to one, Dawson entered.

"What brings you here?" asked Stukely.

"I bade him come," answered Bates. "You need all your witnesses. Here are two of us. There is still another."

"Another?"

"Yes. Yonder he comes. Look at him."

As he spoke Lewson entered the room, Charlotte clinging to his arm.

"Lewson!" exclaimed Stukely, with wildly-staring eyes and quivering lips. "Oh, you cursed villains!"

"Lewson, and alive again," exclaimed that individual. "You hardly looked for me, friend Stukely, after having laid so neat a plan for my taking off. Sharpers and false dice were not enough, it seems, but you must dabble in murder, and so turn your tools into your foes. Take the miserable wretch away," he continued, to Bates and Dawson. "For your lives, see that you guard him closely! He has much to answer for, and I shall hold you responsible if you let him escape."

Stukely was led from the room, with trembling limbs and fallen jaw, by his late associates in crime, such an abject and miserable wreck that even his intended victims could scarcely look upon him otherwise than with pity.

They had a more frightful spectacle soon to behold. The poison which Beverly had rashly swallowed was now flowing like fire through his veins, while his face and limbs grew convulsed, and inch by inch he seemed dying before their faces, consumed by inward pains.

"Ah! that pang!" he cried, in agony. "Where is my wife? Can you forgive me, love?"

"Alas! for what?"

"For meanly dying. Shame, despair, remorse

have been too much for me. I am a dying man; dying—by poison."

"By poison! Oh, fatal deed! Save him! Oh, save him!" cried the distracted wife.

"Alas! that prayer is fruitless. I have lived long enough to ruin you all, and now fly like a coward when there is nothing left for my fatal hand to lose. Charlotte, my sister, can you forgive me?"

"Forgive you! Oh, my poor brother!"

"Lend me your hand, love—so—help me. Oh, for a few short moments, to tell you how my heart bleeds for you! Dying as I am, my deepest pang is for your miseries. Support me, Heaven! Ah! I go,—I die. Oh, mercy! mercy!" With a few more inarticulate words his eyes and lips became fixed, his body fell limply down, death had come,—the career of the gamester was at an end.

DOUGLAS.

BY JOHN HOME.

[JOHN HOME, the leading dramatist of Scottish birth, was born at Leith in 1722. After graduating at the Edinburgh University, he took part in the campaign against the Pretender, and was taken prisoner. He became a minister of the Scottish church in 1747, and shortly afterwards wrote a tragedy named "Agis," which failed at that time to be produced. Subsequently, on a suggestion from the ancient ballad of "Gil Morice," he produced his tragedy of "Douglas," the work on which his fame rests. This play, which was first acted in 1756, gave such offence to the Presbytery that the author resigned his ministry, and went to England, where he became private secretary to the Earl of Bute. He wrote several other plays, all much inferior to "Douglas," and a "History of the Rebellion of 1745." He died in 1808.

Of Home's works, "Douglas" alone for any time held the stage. In this play, which is still classed among the acting drama, the licentiousness of the drama of the Restoration, and the frigid

dramas of Scottish
1721. After gradu-
_____, he took part
_____, and was
_____ of the
_____
_____
_____
_____ "Morien," he produced his tragedy of "_____,"
the work on which his _____ This play,
_____ first _____ in 1736, gave such offence
to _____ that the author resigned his
_____ England, where he became
_____ He _____
_____ of the _____
_____
_____
_____ and was _____ still
_____
of the _____ and the frigid

lifelessness of that of the Addisonian period, are replaced by a purity of sentiment and an emotional warmth and pathos which sufficiently explain the enthusiasm with which it was received. Few plays which have been produced on the English stage have met with a more brilliant success. Home's style is marked by ardor and pathetic feeling, his language is lucid and poetical, and his plots attractive, to which qualities the enduring popularity of his leading dramatic work is due.]

Lady Randolph, the wife of Lord Randolph, a Scottish nobleman of high descent, was the victim of a grief so deep and unceasing that her life seemed but a tale of bitter woe. The true cause of this sorrow none, not even her husband, knew. All supposed that she mourned a favorite brother, who had been slain in battle years before, but this seeming origin of her grief concealed a deeper source of anguish, the more severe that it had to be borne in secret. Lord Randolph loved her with a devoted and jealous affection, and grieved in his turn that his love won no response. His life, in consequence, was so unhappy that he felt tempted to throw himself on the swords of the Danish invaders, who then threatened Scotland, and thus end his suffering existence.

To one person only did the sorrowing lady reveal the secret origin of her woe. This was to a young lady named Anna, her friend and confidante, to whom she told the following touching tale of ancient feud and love's devotion, the source of her life's sorrow.

Her father, Sir Malcolm, of Balarmo, she said, was a stern warrior, fierce in feud and war, and cherishing bitter hatred against Lord Douglas, his hereditary foe. This hatred was not shared by his children, who were of milder and more forgiving disposition. By a strange turn of fortune, Sir Malcolm's son saved in battle the life of young Douglas, the son of his father's foe, and the youthful warriors became such ardent friends that they vowed eternal amity. Young Malcolm, in the warm trust of friendship, so highly praised the beauty of his sister Matilda to the youthful Douglas, that the latter came in disguise to Balarmo, eager to see this charming maiden. She proved as beautiful to his eyes as her brother had painted her, and his heart went out to her with a warm affection which she as fully returned. This love had to be kept secret. None dared reveal the truth to Sir Malcolm. But his son favored the attachment of the youthful lovers, and lent his aid to the ardent desire of Douglas to wed the fair maiden of his heart's choice.

A clandestine marriage took place, and for three weeks the happy couple dwelt in Paradise. But war, with its stern demands, brought their dream of happiness to an end. Douglas was called to fight his father's battles, and Malcolm went with him in spite of his sister's tears.

Hardly had they gone when part of the truth

became known. The stern baron was told that his late visitor was the son of his mortal foe, Lord Douglas. Filled with rage, he sought his daughter, accused her of deceiving him, and of loving one whom it was her hereditary duty to hate, and swore instant death to young Douglas should he ever again dare to set foot within his castle. Not content with this, he drew his sword, and at its point bade his kneeling and weeping daughter to swear that she would never wed with one of that hated name. She took the oath, secure in the fact that the forbidden wedding had already taken place, and trusting that her future happiness would be safe from her father's rage.

The unhappy bride was wofully mistaken. A few days only had passed when a tragic tale was brought to the castle. In a hard-fought battle Malcolm and Douglas had both been slain, her brother and her husband alike being wrested from her at one fell blow. Her grief at this fatal decree of destiny was heart-rending, but it was seemingly for her brother only, and her stern father did not dream that her most bitter tears were shed for one in whose death he openly rejoiced.

But the end of the young wife's troubles had not yet come. A child was born to her, a son, whose face recalled his father's image. Poor waif! his fortune was destined to be a stormy one. The distracted mother did not dare to let her harsh father know the truth. Not while he lived could she safely acknowledge her son. The unfortunate infant was born in a secure retreat, and at once delivered to the nurse, Matilda's only confidante, with instructions to take it to her sister's house, where it was to be reared in secrecy.

A fatal result followed. It was a dark December day. Wind and rain had beaten all night long. The track of the nurse lay across the Carron, which was swollen with the rains. The rushing flood swept the unfortunate woman from her feet, and she and her precious charge were borne away to a watery death. The nurse's body was found the next day, cast up by the subsiding flood, but that of the child had vanished, it doubtless finding a grave in the river's muddy bed.

The story of Matilda's subsequent life Anna did not need to be told. The beautiful young maiden, as all deemed her to be, rendered more interesting to many by her grief, had no lack of suitors for her hand, chief among whom were Lord Randolph and his near kinsman Glenalvon. These two men differed greatly in character. Randolph was all honor, Glenalvon all villany. The widowed bride had no love for either of her suitors, but Glenalvon she despised, and he, despairing of winning her by honorable suit, sought to gain her by abduction. The infamous scheme was frustrated by Randolph, who met the villains and tore their victim from their grasp. In gratitude for his service Matilda consented, at her father's wish, to become his wife, though telling him that she had no love to give.

Years had passed since then. Sir Malcolm had died, and Balarmo had become the home of Lord Randolph and his childless wife. Her grief, reduced by time, still weighed upon her, being added to by the failure of a hope in which she had long indulged, that her son might really have been rescued from the devouring flood, and that she might yet see this darling pledge of her only love.

Glenalvon's designs had not ended with the marriage of Matilda. He had escaped unknown from Lord Randolph's sword, and none knew him for the kidnapper. Should Randolph die he would be heir to his estate, and he hoped, by marrying his widow, to add to this the domain of Balarmo. Cupidity and love thus wrought together in his evil heart. Randolph dead, his widowed wife would have no brother and no near kindred to protect her from her powerful suitor, and the wily villain felt that only the life of his trusting kinsman stood between him and the accomplishment of all his desires.

Such was the condition of affairs at the time our story opens. Glenalvon, deeming that the time for the accomplishment of his dark purpose had now come, placed four murderers in ambush near the castle, concealing them in the bushy borders of a dale through whose winding path the lord of the castle was used to walk. A fortunate chance alone saved Lord Randolph from their swords. They attacked him suddenly, and with such fury that he would have fallen had not a brave young stranger, whom fortune had brought thither at that instant, come to his rescue.

Seeing the old man's imminent danger, the active youth drew his sword, sprang furiously upon the assailants, and used his weapon with such strength and skill that a few thrusts laid the fiercest two of them dead upon the ground. The others fled, and left him master of the blood-stained field.

The stranger had not come alone. A servant had accompanied him. But the coward forsook his master in the fight, leaving him unaided. He returned after victory had declared itself on his master's side, but the indignant youth scornfully dismissed him, and attended Randolph to the castle. Here Lady Randolph, who had learned his service to her lord, gave him the warmest welcome.

"Tell me, dear sir, your name," asked the rescued nobleman. "You answered not when I asked you before." ·

"I am but a low-born man," the stranger modestly replied. "I can boast nothing but a desire to be a soldier, and to win a name in arms."

"You have modesty as well as valor, young sir. Surely one of your high spirit and proud courage need not blush to declare his birth."

"My name is Norval," answered the handsome youth; "on the Grampian hills my father feeds his flocks; a frugal swain, whose only cares were to increase his store, and keep his only son, myself, at home. For I had heard of battles, and I longed to follow to the field some warlike lord. Heaven soon granted what my sire denied. Not many nights ago, a band of robbers from the hills poured on our peaceful vales and swept away our flocks. The shepherds fled in terror, but I, inspired by indignation, followed the foe, marked the road they took, and then pursued them with fifty chosen men. The end is short; we conquered: these are the chieftain's arms I wear to-day. That battle changed my life. I left my father's house, bent on a nobler work than tending sheep, and happy fortune turned my footsteps hither, to save your honored life."

"My brave deliverer! your soul, at least, comes from no lowly strain," exclaimed Lord Randolph. "You shall to the camp with me, and there find nobler foes than wolves and robbers. I will present you to our king, who is ever ready to reward the brave. Next to myself, and equal to Glenalvon, brave youth, shall be your place in honor and command."

"I know not how to thank you," replied Norval, gratefully. "I am rude in speech and manners, and never before stood in so noble a presence. And yet, my lord, I trust not to shame your favor."

"I know you will not," exclaimed Lady Randolph, who had listened with a marked show of emotion. "You shall be my knight; and guard for me, as you have done to-day, Lord Randolph's life."

"Well spoken," answered Randolph. "I go to the camp to-day. Come with me, Norval. There you shall see the chosen warriors of your native land."

"Let us be gone, my lord."

The departure of her husband and his young *protégé* filled Lady Randolph's heart with consuming pain. Some words dropped by her lord vividly recalled to her mind that other occasion, now long years ago, when Douglas and her brother had thus left her, to find their death in the ranks.

"How blest the mother of yon gallant youth!" she plaintively exclaimed. "She had the happy fortune to nurse and rear her darling boy; I gave mine to the roaring waves, to be swept to death."

"Weep not, dear lady," pleaded Anna. "I fancied that valiant stranger had won you from your woe. You gazed on him intently, and with more delight than often brightens your eyes."

"And yet I found in him fuel for sorrow," answered the weeping lady. "I thought that had the son of Douglas lived he might have been, in shape and feature, like this fair youth. I looked on him with something of a mother's fondness, deeming him in years and all endowments what my son might have become. Poor wanderer, I will protect him."

"He will need your aid, dear lady. Your favor and your lord's will rouse up enemies against the youth."

"Glenalvon, yes; he brooks no rival in his kinsman's favor. Yet, bold as he is, and crafty——"

Her words were not finished, for Glenalvon himself entered at that moment, and inquired for Lord Randolph. He declared that he had heard of the base attempt on his kinsman's life, and had surrounded the wood with a band of soldiers; saying that if the villains were taken they should be forced by torture to reveal what foe of Randolph's had hired their swords.

These specious protestations were brought to an end by Lady Randolph, who, first dismissing Anna, told him plainly that she knew him better than he imagined, and bade him cease his base pursuit of herself. If not, she would acquaint Randolph with his dishonorable advances, and have him driven from the castle as an outcast beggar. She further warned him to attempt no treachery against young Norval, the preserver of her husband, for if she heard whisper of it he should find that she was both powerful to protect and to defend.

With these words she left the detected villain, who had heard her with downcast countenance. Not until she had gone did the color return to his pallid cheeks.

"By heaven, I feared at first that she knew all!" he exclaimed. "I am safe yet. As for this new favorite, I dare not strike openly. Ha! I have it! I'll seek the coward slave whom Norval

spurned from him.   Such fellows' rankled bosoms
breed venom.   Doubtless he can be made to serve
me as a useful tool."

While these events were taking place in the
castle, the servants of Lord Randolph had been
searching the wood which had given shelter to
the two escaping villains.   They found there an
old man, who fled like a guilty person on their
approach, but whom they quickly captured.   The
prisoner earnestly denied any knowledge of the
crime, but on searching him they found a number
of valuable jewels concealed in secret places in
his clothing.   They brought him, therefore, before
Lady Randolph, and asked her permission to put
him to the torture, and thus force him to reveal
the truth.

Lady Randolph, on hearing their story, asked
to see the jewels.   But if they had been the eyes of
a basilisk she could not have gazed on them with
more horrified intentness.   On them was engraved
a heart,—the crest of the Douglas.   One glance was
sufficient to tell her a startling story; the jewels
had belonged to her husband, and her own hands
had placed them on the person of her lost child.

Trembling with hope and fear, the deeply agitated lady dismissed the servants; saying that
she would examine the prisoner in private.

"The truth, old man!" she exclaimed.   "Tell
it, or the rack shall wrest it from you.   How came
you by these jewels?"

"Spare me, gentle lady.   These weak old hands

never assailed your lord. Nor are those jewels evidence of crime. Spare me, I pray you."

"The truth,—or death awaits you! Delay not to speak."

The quaking prisoner at this stern command related the story of his life, to which she listened with the most earnest attention. Eighteen years before he had been a tenant of Sir Malcolm, her father. But having fallen into poverty, the servants of that lord had seized his farm, and turned him and his wife and children adrift. The homeless fugitives had found shelter in a hovel by the river's side, where he supported his family by fishing. One stormy night, when the river rushed in torrents past his hut, a cry for help met his ears. He rushed to the water-side, but the person who had uttered the cry was no longer visible. All he saw was a basket, which a whirling eddy had brought into a pool near the bank. This prize he drew ashore, and to his surprise saw nestled there a living infant.

"Living!" exclaimed Lady Randolph, in the deepest emotion. "You did not kill him whom the waves had spared?"

"Kill him, lady? Not for the wealth of kingdoms would I have harmed him!"

"Ha! Then perhaps he still lives."

"Not many days ago he was alive."

"Ah, my heart! Then he has lately died?"

"I have not said so, madam. I hope and pray he lives."

" Where is he, then ?"

" Alas ! I know not where."

" Riddler, you torture me ! Speak out more clearly."

" Let me complete my story, noble lady. That best will answer you."

The old man then proceeded to state that the cradle which held the child held also a store of gold and jewels. This wealth tempted him, in his extreme poverty, to conceal the event, and he resolved to bring the infant up as his own. Leaving the river-side hut, he travelled north with his family, bought flocks and herds, and lived in affluence on the secret hoard obtained from the cradle.

The boy grew in years and beauty, and, as all his own children died, he loved the water-borne waif with a father's fondness, and trained him in all the lessons of honor and virtue. The youth, however, had shown a temper much unlike that of his associate shepherd lads. He was mild with the mild, but fierce with the froward, and thought far more of arms and war than of his pastoral duties. At length a desperate band of robbers descended upon their fields from the mountains, and——

Here Lady Randolph could keep silent no longer, but burst out with,——

" Eternal Providence ! What is your name ?"

" My name is Norval."

"'Tis he ! 'tis himself ! It is my son !" cried

the lady, in a transport of joy. "Oh, sovereign mercy, it was my child I saw! No wonder, Anna, that my bosom burned."

"Thou art the daughter of my ancient master," said old Norval. "But you were a maiden,—the child——"

"Is mine. I was secretly married. My father knew it not; nor must my husband. Can you keep my secret, Norval?"

"With my life. I loved your father, madam, and ever found him kind. He was away, distracted by his son's death, when his servants thrust me from my land. I love his race, and will be faithful to his daughter's wishes."

"If you should meet the youth, still let him call you father."

"Trust me for that, dear lady. I have traced him hither to tell him his true story, and bring him these jewels as aids to find his father. Command me; I am your house's servant."

Lady Randolph now dismissed the old man, first appointing a place where he might abide till sent for, and bidding the servants to set him free.

Then she turned to Anna with a heart that swelled with gladness, and gave vent to her rapturous joy in this discovery. Some instinct had from the first drawn her to the gallant youth who saved her lord from death, but his story of his birth had hindered any suspicion of the happy truth. Now she ardently longed to see him again, to trace in his features the lineaments of

Douglas and herself, and most of all to tell him his true story and clasp him in her arms as his mother.

Anna, while sharing in her joy, warned her not to be hasty. Lord Randolph was of jealous disposition. Should her tenderness show itself in public, before curious observers, deep mischief might come from it.

"The more does it behoove me to declare my son's birth without delay," answered Lady Randolph. "Silence, in cases like this, breeds mischief. I propose to meet him to-night secretly and there tell him his parentage and consult with him. I deem him wise, as was his father, and shall trust to his judgment."

Little did the fond mother dream of the tragic end to her joy which adverse fate was preparing. Glenalvon, in pursuance of his base plot, had sought Norval's dismissed servant, and bribed him to act as his spy and ally. Thus prepared, he sent the fellow to Lady Randolph, bidding him to introduce himself to her as Norval's faithful follower. The scheme proved successful. Lady Randolph intrusted to him the letter she had written to her son, appointing an interview at a secret place in the neighboring forest. This perilous missive the treacherous wretch first bore to Glenalvon, who opened it, read its contents with malignant satisfaction, and showed it to Lord Randolph, whose heart throbbed with jealous rage on finding that his wife had made a secret assignation with the youthful stranger. This mischief done, Glenalvon resealed the letter, and bade the messenger to seek young Norval in the neighboring camp and deliver it to him.

Norval, however, was then at the castle, not the camp, and here met Lady Randolph alone, her heart still enraptured with the joyful tidings she had heard. Her loving eyes, filled with new light, now traced in his ingenuous features the plain likeness of her loved and lost Douglas, and hardly could she desist from clasping him in her arms and claiming him as her son.

"Norval," she said, with difficulty restraining her ardor, "now that lucky chance has left us here alone, I will amaze you with a wondrous tale."

"If there be danger, lady, with the secret, yet tell it; my sword, my life, are yours."

"Know you these gems?" she asked, revealing the jewels taken from the old man.

"Dare I believe my eyes? My father's jewels! How came they here?"

"They were your father's, truly. But not Norval's. This is the tale I promised: you are not Norval's son."

"Not Norval's son!" exclaimed the youth, his eyes distended with surprise.

"No, boy. The blood of shepherds flows not in your veins. You are of noble birth."

"Can I believe this? Norval not my father? Oh, tell me further, lady! Who was my father?"

"Douglas."

"Lord Douglas, whom to-day I saw?"

"No, no, not he, his younger brother. He—ah, unhappy youth!—he fell in battle before you were born."

"Strange tale, indeed! Norval no kin to me—my father dead before I saw the light—Lord Douglas his brother! My mother—does she live?"

"She lives; but wastes her life in constant woe, weeping her husband slain, her infant lost."

"You know my story—my parents—oh, tell me all! Your face confesses that she still is wretched. What can I do to aid her? My heart—my sword——"

"No, no, she now is happy. Your virtue ends her woe. My son! my son!"

"My mother? You?"

"I am your mother, and the wife of Douglas." With tears of joy the happy mother clasped him to her breast, and lavished kisses on his lips.

"Oh, heaven and earth, my mother! Let me kneel——"

"Arise, my son. Ah, how it joys my heart to see in your dear face your father's features! Hear me now. You are the rightful heir of this proud castle and its wide domains. Randolph must yield them to you. If he refuses, Lord Douglas shall protect you."

"Heed it not, mother. To be the son of Douglas is to me inheritance enough. Declare my birth, that men may know me; but let me in the field seek fame and fortune."

"My son, you know not what grave perils surround you. Yonder comes Lord Randolph and Glenalvon. Beware that villain. He craves my husband's lands and title. Your life would stand for little in the way of his ambition."

"Is it so, indeed? Then let him beware of me."

"We must talk further. I have sent you a letter to the camp by your servant's hand appointing a time and place of meeting. Leave me now. Be Norval still, till time is ripe for you to bear the noble name of Douglas."

Little knew the mother and son what venom the serpent had already distilled for their destruction. The letter which Glenalvon had shown to rouse Lord Randolph's jealousy was now followed up by new wiles of the soulless villain. He pointed out to Lord Randolph Norval, who was seemingly stealing from his lady's presence. Her flushed face, nervous preoccupation, and quick withdrawal into the castle, served to add new fuel to her husband's jealousy, which the insidious demon by his side did his utmost to add to.

"You shall see, my lord. We know their place and time of meeting. There we may lurk concealed and witness it."

"She never loved me."

"She betrays you now. Wait, let me accost young Norval with ironical derision. If he be humble still, he'll shrink before me. But if he be the favorite of the first of Caledonia's dames, he'll turn upon me as the lion turns upon the hunter's spear."

Glenalvon well knew the spirit of the young man, and with half-hidden insults soon stirred him up to such anger that, in the end, Norval hotly drew his sword and bade him defend himself.

At this moment Lord Randolph, who had remained in concealment during the angry colloquy, stepped forth and sternly bade them to desist, demanding the cause of their quarrel. Norval declared that he had been bitterly insulted, and much as he esteemed Lord Randolph, could not forgive Glenalvon.

"You may find better work for your swords at present," replied Randolph, sternly. "Keep them for your country's foe. Repel the invader, then decide your private quarrel."

"Be it so," they both answered.

Glenalvon had no intention to fight with the high-spirited youth. His aim was but to add fuel to Lord Randolph's jealousy. At the time appointed for the meeting of Lady Randolph with her son, he led her husband from the castle to the leafy covert in which they designed to conceal themselves.

By chance, on their way thither, old Norval, who was lurking near by, heard part of their conversation, and listened in affright to their words. He heard them but imperfectly, but found that they were speaking in threatening tones of his reputed son and Lady Randolph.

They claimed to have made a wonderful discovery, and vowed revenge.

Shortly afterwards, the old man, hastening from that spot, met young Norval—or Douglas, rather—and told him what he had learned. " Revenge !—for what?" asked the startled youth. "For being Sir Malcolm's heir," replied the old man, as he hastened to confirm what Lady Randolph had already revealed. Douglas listened in mingled joy and sorrow to this confirmation of his mother's story, and declared that he would not forsake him whom he had always known as a father, whatever might betide. As for his noble mother, he continued, he awaited her at that moment, and was eager to hear and be governed by her counsel. He, therefore, requested old Norval to leave him, as his interview with his mother must be private.

The departure of the old man was quickly followed by the entrance of Lady Randolph, who tenderly embraced her son, and asked him why his face wore so grave an aspect. He replied by repeating the tale which he had just heard, that Randolph and Glenalvon had spoken of a strange discovery and vowed revenge.

She heard him in trembling fear. Like him, she could conceive but one origin for their threats, that they had learned the secret of his birth, and were determined to remove from their path this rightful claimant to the estate of Balarmo. She bade her son fly to the camp, show Lord Douglas the jewels, tell him the story he had learned, and request his aid and protection. Before parting, she begged him to abate his thirst for war, for she feared that she might lose him as she had his father. These words were wasted on the young man's ardent spirit. He vowed that only on the invaders' heads could he prove his high descent, and embracing her with a warmth born of filial love, he hastened from her presence.

At the same moment Randolph and Glenalvon burst from their ambush, and rushed out before the frightened woman, who fled in dismay.

"Where is he? Gone?" cried Randolph, in jealous fury. "Stay, Glenalvon, I go alone. It never shall be said that I took odds in combat. Leave me to my revenge."

He rushed away in pursuit of Douglas, and in a minute more loud voices and the clashing of swords could be heard. Glenalvon listened with a face of wily treachery.

"Now is my time," he cried. "A double slaughter clears my path. I'll take them unawares."

Drawing his sword, he hurried towards the sounds of combat. In a minute more Lady Randolph returned. The clash of swords had caught her ears, and she came flying back, faint and breathless.

"Lord Randolph, hear me!" she cried. "Take all my wealth, but spare, oh, spare my son!"

The sounds of battle ceased as suddenly as they

had begun. As the mother's eyes looked distractedly towards the locality of the duel, Douglas returned, weak and bleeding, but with a sword in each hand.

"My mother's voice!" he cried. "I can protect you still."

"He lives! he lives!" she exclaimed, in joyful accents. "Surely I saw you fall."

"It was Glenalvon. I mastered Randolph: this is his sword. But as I did so the villain came behind me,—and I slew him."

"Behind you! You are wounded? Ah, me, how pale you grow!"

"I feel a little faintness; it soon will pass," said Douglas, leaning on his sword.

"Your pallid lips!—your flowing blood! Oh, Douglas, Douglas, the hand of death is on you!"

"Dear mother. Ah! I fear that we must part. Oh, had I fallen as my brave fathers fell, I could have welcomed death! But thus to perish, by a villain's hand——"

He reeled with these words and fell prostrate, while his despairing mother sank with streaming eyes on her knees beside him.

"My eyes that gaze on you grow dim apace: my mother—oh, my mother——" A gasp stopped his utterance, and his eyes closed in death, while with a cry of agony the tortured woman threw herself upon his body, clasping it wildly in her arms.

At the same moment Lord Randolph and Anna entered, in earnest conversation.

5*

"Her son! Your words have pierced my heart!" he said. "Oh, if he but survives the traitor's sword——"

"Look there, my lord!"

"The mother and her son! Both dead? How cursed I am!"

"No, no, my lady lives!"

Their words seemed to pierce the numbed senses of the distracted mother. She struggled to her feet and tossed her arms wildly in the air, exclaiming,—

"My son! my son! my beautiful and brave! How proud I was of you and of your valor! Now all my hopes, with you, are dead. A little while I was a wife! a mother not so long! What am I now? What shall I be? My son, my husband, call me! Yes, I hear, I come!"

Springing to her feet, she ran distractedly from the spot. Anna followed her, at Lord Randolph's request. While the nobleman stood there, torn with sad emotions, old Norval entered, and seeing what had happened, burst into a storm of grief, flinging himself madly on the ground beside the dead body of him whom he had cherished as a son.

"My lord! my lord!" cried Anna, who now returned, her eyes distended with mortal fright.

"Speak: what new horror! Matilda!"

"Is no more. She flew like lightning up yon rocky hill, and from its precipice leaped headlong down, to dreadful death!"

"Wretch that I am, 'twas I that drove her

to it!" exclaimed the half-maddened nobleman. "Would that I had died too! Mother and son, both slain by that base villain!—by me rather; for 'twas my jealousy that wrought their death! What is there left for me, but in the battle's van to seek release from life's sad bonds? I go; the foe that checks me there must threaten worse than death!"

And with slow steps and bent head the sad old nobleman withdrew from that scene of death, feeling that life for him had ceased, and that he who should first plunge a sword into his breast would be his dearest friend.

SHE STOOPS TO CONQUER.

BY OLIVER GOLDSMITH.

[OF the literary skill of. Oliver Goldsmith we have no occasion to speak. Whatever he touched he adorned; and his writings, alike in poetry, the drama, fiction, essay, and other fields of literature, are among the choicest legacies of thought from the eighteenth century to the nineteenth.

This distinguished author was born at Pallas, in Longford, Ireland, in 1728, obtained his education at Trinity College, Dublin, and passed an adventurous life, in which he showed a much better faculty in getting rid of money than in getting it. After trying his hand at almost every varity of literary production, and always with success from a literary point of view, he ventured into the field of the drama; his first play, " The Good-Natured Man," being produced in 1768, with some success. In 1773, a year only before his death, appeared his great dramatic triumph, " She Stoops to Conquer," which still remains one of the most popular of English comedies. As a man, Goldsmith was thoughtless and improvident, and spent the most of his life in pecuniary diffi-

56

culties; but he was warm-hearted and generous, and full of love and charity for his fellow-beings. As a writer, humor and pathos are deftly mingled in his style, which has a native charm which few writers have equalled, and which will make him a favorite while English literature survives.]

In a roomy hill-side mansion of Southern England, at a considerable distance from the metropolis, dwelt a genial but old-fashioned country squire named Hardcastle, with a family consisting of his wife, a woman largely made up of whims and follies; his daughter Kate, a handsome and sensible young lady; his wife's ward Miss Neville, Kate's bosom friend; and his step-son, Tony Lumpkin, his mother's darling, but an unmanageable cub, who spent his days in low company at roadside inns. As for the young ladies, Mr. Hardcastle and his wife had laid plans for their future happiness, or misery, as it might prove. The fortune of Miss Neville consisted principally of jewels, which had been left in trust to Mrs. Hardcastle, who had firmly made up her mind to keep them in the family. With this intent she had arranged in her own fancy a match between her lady ward and her son Tony. The courting, however, was principally done by the mother, her undutiful son having little fancy for being tied for life to a fine lady. Miss Neville, for purposes of her own, affected to favor the suit. She was really in love with a young gentleman of very different calibre from Tony, but felt it necessary to cajole the old lady, until she could get her jewels into her own possession.

While Mrs. Hardcastle was thus arranging a marriage for the ward, Mr. Hardcastle was doing the same thing for the daughter. He had selected a suitor much more likely to prove agreeable to the young lady,—Charles Marlow, the son of his old friend, Sir Charles Marlow,—a handsome and cultivated young gentleman, but noted for his exceeding bashfulness with ladies of reputation, though he was credited with assurance enough with women of a lower grade in society. He was now on his way to Mr. Hardcastle's house, in company with his intimate friend, Mr. Hastings, Miss Neville's lover, who had joined him with the warm desire to see his lady love.

Kate Hardcastle had made the following compact with her father. A year or two's residence in London had filled her head with fashionable ideas, and she was much fonder of "gauze and French frippery" than her old-fashioned parent approved of. She had therefore agreed that, if he would let her dress to please herself in the morning, she would wear a housewife's dress to please him in the evening, and change her fashionable gayety at the same time for the plainest country manners, if he desired. This compact was destined to give rise to the strangest series of misunderstandings, and produce results of which the contracting parties never dreamed.

Mr. Hardcastle, for reasons of his own, had kept secret from his daughter the expected arrival of young Marlow, and the purpose of his coming. Not until the afternoon of the day in which the lover was looked for did he advise Kate of the plan he had laid for her future. She had every reason, though, he told her, to be satisfied. Mr. Marlow was young, brave, generous, and handsome, a scholar and gentleman; his only drawback being that he was one of the most bashful persons in the world. This impediment to the freedom of courtship was not much to the taste of the young lady; she had no fancy for a timid and sheepish lover,—but a polished London gentleman in that country district!—that was a prize worth having, and timidity was a fault that might be cured. On the whole, she rather approved of the situation.

Kate lost no time in telling her friend Constance of the interesting event to take place that evening, and threw her into as great a flutter as herself, for Miss Neville knew that Marlow was the intimate friend of her lover, Mr. Hastings, and her heart throbbed with joy at the hope that they might come together. His advent might create awkward complications, it was true; Mrs. Hardcastle was lynx-eyed in her matrimonial plans for her dear Tony; but something might arise to overcome her vigilance and set her ward at liberty, and the hopeful young lady was quite willing to trust to the chapter of chances.

While Kate and Constance were in such a state of mind over the news they had received, an event of the utmost importance to our story was taking place a few miles away. In an ale-house called the Three Pigeons sat Tony Lumpkin, at a table around which were ranged several shabby companions, of the sort which he preferred as associates, while on the board before them was a plentiful supply of punch and tobacco. Tony occupied the head of the table, as the master spirit of the company, and had just finished a rollicking drinking song when the landlord entered and informed him that there were two gentlemen in a post-chaise at the door, who had lost their way, and were making inquiries about Mr. Hardcastle.

"Do they look like Londoners?" asked Tony.

"I'd take 'em for Frenchmen," said the landlord.

"As sure as maybe, one of them is the gentleman that's coming down to court my sister. Show them in, Stingo. Gentlemen, just you step out awhile; I'll be with you in the squeezing of a lemon."

In a moment Tony was left alone. He stood in an expectant attitude, muttering sourly to himself.

"Father-in-law has been calling me whelp and hound this half year. Now, if I pleased, I could be revenged on the old grumbletonian. Ecod, I've half a mind to try; he can't out me out of my fortune for a joke."

He was interrupted in his soliloquy by the entrance of Marlow and Hastings, two young gentlemen of good figure and handsome feature, who were attired in the most fashionable cut of travelling costume. They stood talking over the situation, Tony gathering from their words that they were completely at a loss to tell where they were.

"You are asking for a Mr. Hardcastle, I hear," he remarked. "Pray, is not this same Hardcastle a cross-grained, old-fashioned, whimsical fellow, with an ugly face; a daughter, who is a tall, trolloping, talkative May-pole; and a son, a pretty, well-bred, agreeable youth, that everybody is fond of?"

"Why, as for the old gentleman, we can't say," answered Marlow. "But we have been told that the daughter is well-bred and beautiful; the son an awkward booby, reared at his mother's apron-string, and spoiled by her folly."

"He-he-hem!" stammered Tony, not quite relishing this picture. "Well, gentlemen, all I have to say is that you won't reach Mr. Hardcastle's house this night; unless you want to make a road over Quagmire Marsh. Stingo, tell the gentlemen the way to Mr. Hardcastle's."

The landlord, admonished by a wink from Tony, laid out such an impassable route that it seemed madness to attempt it, and the travellers in despair began to talk of seeking quarters at the Three Pigeons for the night. But Tony quickly advised them that there was no hope in that quarter, the only spare bed in the house having three lodgers already.

"Let me see, gentlemen," he continued. "What if you go on a mile farther, to the Buck's Head; the old Buck's Head on the hill, one of the best inns in the whole county?"

"You ben't sending 'em to your father's as an inn, be you?" said the landlord, in an aside to Tony.

"Mum, you fool! Let them find that out," whispered Tony. "You have only to keep straight on, gentlemen, till you come to a large old house by the road-side, with a pair of buck's horns over the door. That's the sign. Drive up the yard, and call stoutly about you."

"Sir, we are obliged," said Hastings. "Our servants can't miss the way."

"I warn you, though, that the landlord is rich and going to retire from business," continued Tony; "so he wants to be thought a gentleman, he! he! he! He'll be for giving you his company; and ecod, if you mind him, he'll persuade you that his mother was an alderman, and his aunt a justice of the peace."

"A troublesome old blade, to be sure," added the landlord; "but keeps as good wines and beds as any in the county."

"Why, if he supplies us with these, we shall ask no more. Turn to the right did you say?"

"No, no; straight forward. I'll step out myself, and show you a piece of the way."

While the mischievous young rascal was thus planting the seeds of future misconception, his worthy father-in-law was engaged in training in table exercises a corps of servants taken from the plow and the barn-yard. His efforts in this direction were far from successful; he found the rustics incorrigible dunces; and in the midst of his lessons a post-chaise drove into the yard, and the expected guests were shown into the house.

The two young gentlemen, full of the idea that they were in an inn, were ushered into the room which Mr. Hardcastle and the servants had just vacated. They gazed approvingly at its handsome and comfortable appointments, though with the fear that they would be made to pay for all this elegance in their bill. From admiring the room, they fell to talking of more personal subjects, the question of Marlow's diffidence being broached.

"I don't know how, but a single glance from a pair of fine eyes robs me of all my courage," he remarked. "An impudent fellow may counterfeit modesty; but I'll be hanged if a modest man can ever counterfeit impudence."

"I don't understand you, man. I have heard you lavish hosts of fine things on the bar-maid of an inn."

"Your fine ladies petrify me, George. To me, a modest woman, dressed out in all her finery, is the most tremendous object of the whole creation. This stammer in my address, and this awkward—— Pshaw! this fellow here to interrupt us!"

The *fellow* alluded to was Mr. Hardcastle himself, who entered the room in a very gracious manner, bidding his guests heartily welcome to his fireside. The young travellers, thinking him but a garrulous landlord, paid little attention to what he said, and went on to talk of their purpose in visiting his house as freely as if he were not in the room.

"Pray be under no restraint in this house," said the surprised old gentleman. "This is Liberty Hall. You may do just as you please here."

The visitors took him at his word, for when he began to tell one of the long-winded military anecdotes of which he had an abundant store at his command, they chatted on without listening to a word he said. Marlow at length interrupted him with,—

"What, my good friend, if you gave us a glass of punch in the mean time? It would help us to carry on the siege with vigor."

"Punch, sir! This is the most unaccountable kind of modesty I ever met with," said Hardcastle to himself.

"Yes, sir, punch. This is Liberty Hall, you know."

This was but the beginning of Mr. Hardcastle's bewilderment. From punch they turned to the question of provender, demanding to know what he had in the house for supper; and when he, after some persuasion, sent for the bill of fare, one did not like this, and the other could not bear that, till their host stood overwhelmed by their impudence.

"I'm sorry, gentlemen," he broke out at last, "that I have nothing you like; but if there be anything you have a particular fancy to——"

"Why, sir," interrupted Marlow, "your bill of fare is so exquisite that any one part of it is fully as good as another. Send us what you please. So much for supper: and now to see that our beds are aired and properly taken care of."

"I entreat you, leave all that to me. You shall not stir a step."

"Leave it to you? No, indeed; I always look to these things myself."

"I must insist, sir, that you make yourself easy on that head."

"You see I'm resolved on it," said Marlow; adding in an aside, "A very troublesome old fellow, this!"

"Well, sir, I'm resolved at least to attend you," answered Hardcastle; continuing to himself, "This may be modern modesty; but I never saw anything look so like old-fashioned impudence."

They left the room together, Hastings remaining behind.

"This fellow's civilities begin to grow troublesome," he said. "Yet they are meant to please——

Ha! what do I see? Miss Neville, by all that's happy!"

"My dear George!" exclaimed Miss Neville, who entered the room at that moment. "This is a happy meeting, indeed."

"And a surprising one. I never dreamed of meeting my dear Constance at an inn."

"An inn!" she echoed, in surprise. "Mr. Hardcastle's house an inn! What gave you such a strange idea?"

"Mr. Marlow and I were sent here as to an inn. A young fellow, a mile below here, told us——"

"Ha! ha! ha! that is one of my hopeful cousin's tricks."

"What! the lout whom your aunt intends for you, and of whom I have had such apprehensions?"

"You need not, George. You'd adore the fellow if you knew how heartily he despises me."

"An inn! Ha! ha! ha! But Marlow must be kept in ignorance. If he knew the truth his modesty would drive him out of the house within the hour. We must keep up the deception."

"But how? Miss Hardcastle has been out walking, but will be here in a few minutes. Is this Mr. Marlow, now?"

Marlow entered as she spoke, complaining of the annoying attentions of the landlord, whom he found to be a troublesome old bore. He was somewhat taken aback on being introduced to Miss Neville, and told that Miss Hardcastle had stopped at the inn with her, and that he would see her in a moment. Every spark of his assurance died out at the thought of meeting her thus suddenly, and he was only kept from taking to flight by Hastings' promise to support him.

In the midst of their conference Miss Hardcastle entered, in a walking dress. Miss Neville at once introduced her to the gentlemen, and a conversation ensued, during which Marlow never once lifted his eyes to the young lady's face, and hardly spoke a word except as prompted by his more collected friend.

"Miss Hardcastle, I see that you and Mr. Marlow are going to be very good company," said Hastings, at length. "We are only in your way."

"Not in the least!" exclaimed Marlow, hastily. "We like your company of all things.—Zounds, George," he whispered to him, "you won't go?"

"Consider, man, Miss Neville and I must have a little *tête-à-tête* of our own," and Hastings wickedly walked out with his inamorata, leaving Marlow in a fit of the most embarrassing nervousness.

An amusing conversation followed, in which Miss Hardcastle led, and Marlow stumblingly endeavored to reply.

"You were observing, sir," she went on, after some ridiculous remark on the part of the gentleman, "that in this age of hypocrisy—something about hypocrisy."

"Yes, madam; in this age of hypocrisy, there

are few who, upon strict inquiry, do not—
a-a-a——"

"I understand you perfectly, sir."

"That is more than I do myself," said Marlow,
in an aside. "Yes, madam, as I was saying——
But I am sure I tire you."

"Not in the least, sir; there's something so
agreeable and spirited in your manner; such life
and force; pray, sir, go on."

"I was saying," continued Marlow, his nervousness increasing, "that there are some occasions,—
when a want of courage destroys all the—and
puts us—upon a-a-a——"

"I agree with you entirely."

"Yes, madam, morally speaking. But I see
Miss Neville expecting us in the next room. We
must not detain her. Shall I have the honor to
attend you, madam?"

"I'll follow, sir."

"This pretty, smooth dialogue has done for me,"
groaned Marlow to himself, as he escaped from
the room.

"Ha! ha! ha!" laughed Miss Hardcastle, when
he had vanished, "did any one ever talk such
sober, sentimental nonsense? And he never
looked in my face the whole time! Yet he would
do pretty well, only for his ridiculous bashfulness.
If I could only teach him a little confidence,
now!"

Marlow had fibbed slightly; Miss Neville was
not in the next room. She and Hastings had

passed on to another apartment, in which they
found Mrs. Hardcastle and Tony. Miss Neville
introduced her lover to the old lady, and left them
engaged in conversation, while she devoted herself to Tony, who was anything but pleased with
her attentions.

"It's very hard to be followed about so," he
broke out at length, in a pet. "Ecod, I've not a
place left me in the house now, but the stable."

"Cousin Tony is generous," said the teasing
young lady. "He falls out before faces that he
may be forgiven in private."

"That's a confounded—crack!" said Tony,
testily.

Mrs. Hardcastle, who had been uneasily watching them, now came to the rescue, declaring that
there never was a pair better matched by nature.
Her dear Tony was the picture of his cousin even
in height. To prove this, she set them back to
back; when the mischievous young scamp, whose
temper was much ruffled, gave the young lady
such a crack with the back of his head that the
air before her danced with stars. This perverse
behavior was too much for the doting mother.
She left the room in tears, followed by Miss
Neville, while Hastings proceeded to lecture her
graceless son severely on his bad behavior.

The lecture proved not very successful. Tony
gave Hastings very freely his opinion of his
cousin, whom he spoke of as a bitter, cantankerous
toad, full of tricks, and her beauty all made up.

"What would you say to a friend who would take this bitter bargain off your hands?" asked Hastings.

"Where is there such a friend? Who would take her?" demanded Tony.

"He stands before you. If you but assist me, I'll engage to whip her off to France, and you shall never hear more of her."

"Assist you? Ecod, I will, to the last drop of my blood! I'll clap a pair of horses to your chaise that shall trundle you off in a twinkling; and maybe get you a part of her fortune besides, in jewels, that you little dream of."

"My dear squire, this looks like a lad of spirit."

"Come along, then, and you shall see more of my spirit before you have done with me," and Tony led the way from the room, singing an ale-house ditty as he went.

Mrs. Hardcastle's undutiful son was as good as his word. The young scamp had keys to all his mother's drawers, which he had often used for the purpose of helping himself to funds for his ale-house frolics. By their aid he now quickly made himself master of the casket containing Miss Neville's jewels, which he delivered into Hastings' hands.

While the worthy pair were thus helping themselves by what Tony called "the rule of thumb," Miss Neville, who had laid her plans with her lover, was seeking to obtain her jewels by the more honorable method of persuasion. She found

Mrs. Hardcastle, however, hard to convince. " It will be time enough for jewels twenty years hence. Jewels are not worn at present. Yours are only a parcel of old-fashioned rose and table-cut things." These and other reasons she gave for not delivering them, ending by saying, " they may be missing, for aught I know to the contrary."

" Tell her so at once," whispered the mischievous Tony, who had come into the room during this conversation. " Tell her they're lost, and call me to bear witness. It's the only way to quiet her."

This suggestion was accepted by the astute guardian. She declared that the jewels *were* missing; an assertion which Tony professed he was ready to take oath to. The old lady acknowledged, however, that she was responsible for their value, and said that if Constance was so anxious for jewels, she would lend her her own garnets.

Mrs. Hardcastle left the room to procure these, and her tricky son took advantage of the opportunity to bid Miss Neville hasten to her lover, who would tell her something to her satisfaction about the jewels. " Vanish !" he cried. " He has them. She's here, and has missed them already."

Miss Neville hastened from the room, at the same moment that Mrs. Hardcastle entered in a panic of excitement. " Thieves ! robbers ! We are cheated, robbed, plundered !" she cried.

" What's the matter, mamma ?" asked Tony, innocently.

"My bureau has been broken open and the jewels taken! We are robbed, undone!"

"Oh! is that all! Ha! ha! ha! by the laws, I never saw it better acted in my life! Ecod, I thought you was ruined in earnest; ha! ha! ha!"

"Why, boy, I *am* ruined in earnest. The jewels are stolen, I say."

"Stick to that; ha! ha! ha! stick to that; I'll bear witness, you know; call me to bear witness."

"My dearest Tony, hear me. By all that's precious, the jewels are really gone."

"Ha! ha! ha! mamma. I know who took them well enough; ha! ha! ha!"

And the mischievous rogue kept up his provoking show of belief in her skill as an actress, till the badgered woman finally drove him from the room, calling him fool and unfeeling brute, to all of which he returned the same provoking answer, "I can bear witness to that."

While the affairs of Hastings and Miss Neville were making this favorable progress, those of Marlow and Miss Hardcastle had reached an interesting phase. In compliance with her compact with her father, Kate had laid aside her fashionable attire, and put on a plain housewife's dress, in which garb she presented herself for his approval. He thanked her for her obedience to his wishes, and entered into a conversation with her about her lover, in which it soon appeared that there was a decided difference of opinion. Kate described him as the most bashful man it had ever been her fortune to meet; her father, as "the most impudent piece of brass that ever spoke with a tongue."

"He met me with a respectful bow, a stammering voice, and a look fixed on the ground," she affirmed.

"He met me with a loud voice, a lordly air, and a familiarity that made my blood freeze," he replied; "and interrupted my best stories by asking me if I was not a good hand at making punch."

"One of us must certainly be mistaken," answered Kate.

"If he be the impudent fellow he seems, I am determined he shall never have my consent."

"And if he prove the sullen thing I found him, he shall never have mine. But as one of us must be mistaken, what if we go on to make further discoveries?"

"Depend on't, I'm in the right," declared Mr. Hardcastle, positively.

"And depend on't, I'm not in the wrong," answered his daughter, as positively.

Kate Hardcastle was destined soon to behold her lover in a new light. Still full of the idea that Mr. Hardcastle's house was an inn, he chanced to see the young lady in her plain attire, and, misled by his mistaken fancy, asked her maid if this were not the bar-maid. His error was quickly reported by the maid to her mistress, who resolved to take advantage of it, remembering Marlow's reputation for gallantry with women in that rank of life.

"Can you act your part, and disguise your voice, so that he may not discover you?" asked the maid.

"Never fear me. I think I know the true bar cant. 'Did your honor call? Attend the Lion there. Pipes and tobacco for the Angel. The Lamb has been outrageous this half hour.'"

"That will do, madam. And here he comes."

The maid hastened away, leaving her mistress to practise her new lesson on Marlow, who just then entered the room, grumbling to himself at the annoyance which he received from the assiduous attentions of the host and hostess.

He walked about in a musing humor. "As for Miss Hardcastle, she's too grave and sentimental for me."

"Did you call, sir? Did your honor call?" asked the seeming bar-maid.

"No, child—— Besides," he resumed, "from the glimpse I had of her I think she squints."

"I am sure, sir, the bell rang."

"No, no—— Well, I've pleased my father by coming. To-morrow, I'll please myself by returning."

"Perhaps the other gentleman called, sir."

"No, no, I tell you." He now for the first time lifted his eyes to her face, and was struck by her modest beauty. "Yes, I think I did call. I wanted—I wanted—— I vow, child, you are vastly handsome."

"Oh! la, sir, you'll make one ashamed."

The conversation thus auspiciously begun went

on at a rattling pace. All Marlow's diffidence
vanished, and in a very few minutes he was making an earnest show of love to the supposed bar-
maid, whose beauty, in her neat housewife's dress,
was certainly very attractive.

"I'm sure you didn't talk this way to Miss
Hardcastle," she protested. "I'll warrant me you
looked as dashed before her as if she was a justice
of the peace."

"In awe of her, child! A mere awkward,
squinting thing! No, no; I find you don't know
me. I merely rallied her a little."

"Oh, then, sir, you are a favorite among the
ladies?"

"A great favorite, my dear. At the ladies'
club in town, I'm called their agreeable Rattle.
Rattle, child, is not my real name, but one I'm
known by. My name is——" He attempted to
kiss her, but found herself modestly repulsed.

Marlow, however, as the conversation continued,
found his fancy so enslaved by the beauty and
vivacity of the seeming bar-maid that he went
beyond the boundaries of discretion, seizing her
hand, and attempting to take by force the kiss
she had refused. At this moment, to his confusion,
he was interrupted by the sudden entrance of Mr.
Hardcastle. He dropped the young lady's hand,
and left the room in haste.

"So, miss, is this your *modest* lover?" exclaimed
the astounded old gentleman. "Kate, Kate, are
you not ashamed to deceive your father so?"

"Believe me, papa, he is still the modest man I took him for: you shall be convinced of it."

"Convinced! Would you drive me mad? You may like this impudence, and call it modesty; but —— Why I saw him seize your hand and haul you about like a milkmaid! The brazen rascal shall never be son-in-law of mine!"

"Give me but an hour to convince you."

"An hour be it, then. But all must be fair and open. No trifling with your father, Kate."

"Your wishes shall be my commands, dear papa."

The hour's probation thus agreed upon proved to be one that was crowded with events. The first was in the form of a letter from Sir Charles Marlow to Mr. Hardcastle, saying that he would be there that evening, as he intended to take the road shortly after his son. The second was an awkward mistake in regard to Miss Neville's jewels. Hastings, having his hands full of preparations for the elopement, sent the casket to Marlow to keep for him, as their baggage was in his care. Marlow, who deemed the seat of a post-chaise at an inn-door not a very safe receptacle for valuables, sent the casket by a servant to the hostess for safe keeping. Thus, by this odd misunderstanding, the jewels fell again into Mrs. Hardcastle's hands, who took them into custody with an eagerness which almost included the servant who brought them.

Meanwhile matters were rapidly advancing to

a climax between Mr. Hardcastle and his deceived and easy-going guest. While Marlow was cosily seated in his host's favorite easy-chair, his mind full of the beauty, grace, and vivacity of the charming little bar-maid, Mr. Hardcastle entered in a testy humor, exclaiming that he no longer knew his own house, it had been so overturned by the aggressive impertinence of his guests.

An exciting conversation took place between him and Marlow, in which they were sadly at cross-purposes. Marlow indignantly demanded what more his host required of him. If he did not drink himself, he had given orders to his servants not to spare the cellar, and he sent for one of them in proof that the fellows were already comfortably drunk.

This added fire to the fuel of Mr. Hardcastle's wrath, and he ordered the guest to leave the house at once. Marlow replied that he would do nothing of the sort; the house was his own while he chose to pay his way in it.

"It is yours, sir!" exclaimed the host; "then perhaps you claim the furniture as well? Here is a pair of silver candlesticks; there a fire-screen; here a mahogany table,—you may take a fancy to them, perhaps."

"Say no more, sir," cried Marlow, now in a passion; "bring me your bill; let's make no more words about it."

"My bill, young man! Mercy on me, from his father's letter I was taught to expect a well-bred, modest man as a visitor, instead of a coxcomb and a bully. But Sir Charles will be here presently, and shall hear my opinion of it all." And the old gentleman stamped from the room in a rage, leaving his guest in a very uneasy state of mind.

Mr. Hardcastle's last words were certainly not those of an innkeeper. But if his house were not an inn, what was it doing with a bar-maid? Marlow felt that he must know the truth at once, and fortunately for him Miss Hardcastle entered at the height of his dilemma. His first question convinced her that he suspected his error, and she made a virtue of necessity by undeceiving him, laughing at him heartily for mistaking one of the best manor houses in the county for an inn. As for herself, she declared that she was a poor relation of the family, who kept the keys and looked after the comfort of the guests.

This information threw Marlow into a sad stew. To mistake Mr. Hardcastle's house for an inn, and order his father's old friend about as an innkeeper! The story would surely get afloat, and he would be the laugh of all London.

"What a set of blunders have I made!" he exclaimed. "My stupidity saw everything the wrong way. I even mistook your manner for the alluring arts of a bar-maid. It is over. This house I no more show *my* face in."

"I'm sure I should be sorry if you left the family on my account," whimpered Kate, artfully, pretending to cry. "I'm sure I should be sorry if people said anything amiss, since I have no fortune but my character."

"She weeps! By Heaven, this mark of tenderness touches me!" said Marlow to himself. "Excuse me, my lovely girl, you are the only part of the family I leave with reluctance. Dream not that I could ever harbor a thought to your harm."

Their conversation went on, Marlow being more and more attracted by her affected simplicity and grief, till he was obliged to leave the room lest his feelings should carry him too far. As for Miss Hardcastle, his artless show of affection filled her heart with pleasure, and she determined that he should not go if she had the power to detain him.

Hastings's affairs were rapidly getting into as great a complication as those of his friend. Through one blunder the stolen jewels had been returned to Mrs. Hardcastle's hands. A still more awkward blunder was to follow. While Miss Neville and Tony were playing at love-making, to deceive the old lady, a servant entered and delivered the young squire a letter, which Miss Neville recognized at once to be in the handwriting of her lover. Here was new danger. Tony's education in the reading of manuscript was decidedly lacking, and he was in the habit of having his mother read all his correspondence. The alarmed young lady drew Mrs. Hardcastle aside on pretence of something very amusing to tell her, to give Tony an opportunity to read his missive, but he became so puzzled over the crabbed writing that his mother anxiously offered her assistance.

"Let me read it," exclaimed Miss Neville, hastily, snatching it from his hand. "Nobody reads a cramped hand better than I. Do you know who it is from?"

"Can't tell, except from Dick Ginger, the feeder."

"Ay, so it is." She pretended to read. "'Dear Squire,—Hoping that you're in health, as I am at present. The gentlemen of the Shake-bag Club has cut the gentlemen of the Goose-green quite out of feather. The odds—um—odd battle—um—long fighting—um——' Here, it's all about cocks and fighting. Put it up; it's of no consequence."

"Of no consequence! Why, I would not lose the rest of it for a guinea!" exclaimed Tony. "Here, mother, do you make it out."

The mischief was done. Miss Neville recoiled in dismay as her aunt read a letter from Hastings to Tony, to the effect that he was waiting for Miss Neville with a post-chaise at the bottom of the garden, but that he needed the fresh horses, as promised. Despatch was necessary, for suspicion might at any moment be aroused.

To use a homely phrase, "the fat was all in the fire." Mrs. Hardcastle broke out furiously upon her lady ward, and her son as well. So they were plotting together to deceive her! She vowed that she would not be longer pestered by such uncertain baggage, but would at once convey the tricky young lady to her Aunt Pedigree, whom she could depend on to keep her from all runaway lovers. With these words she ran from the room in a rage, declaring that the coach should be got ready instantly, and ordering her deceitful son to prepare himself to accompany them as a mounted guard.

Here was a fine end to a promising scheme! Miss Neville turned waspishly on Tony, and charged him with ruining her; but he retorted that she had only her own extra cleverness, with her Shake-bags and Goose-greens, to thank for her trouble. Hastings and Marlow entered a moment afterwards, and both set so violently upon him as the cause of all their difficulties that for once the mischievous young rogue found himself at a loss for an answer.

As for Mrs. Hardcastle, she was in serious earnest. Late in the evening as it was, she had the horses harnessed to the coach, and sent a servant to her ward, ordering her to prepare for a journey instantly, as she was determined they should set out at once.

"I shall be three years a prisoner!" exclaimed Miss Neville, with tears of vexation in her eyes. "My dear George, I can but trust to your esteem and constancy to wait for me during that dreary interval till the law sets me free."

"How can I bear this?" he answered. "Happiness robbed from me when in my very hands! You see, young sir, what a strait your folly and love of amusement have got us all in."

"Ecod, I have it!" cried Tony, with a sudden inspiration. "I'll bring you all out right yet. My boots there, ho! Meet me two hours hence at the bottom of the garden; and if you don't find Tony Lumpkin a more good-natured fellow than you thought for, I'll give you leave to take my best horse, and Bet Bouncer, the girl of my heart, into the bargain. My boots, ho!" And he hurried from the room, leaving them all in a state of new hope.

That Tony was as good as his word need scarcely be said. Two hours afterwards Hastings found him at the place appointed,—the bottom of the garden,—bespattered like one who had just ended a long and muddy journey.

"Five and twenty miles in two hours and a half is no such bad driving," he said. "The poor beasts have smoked for it. Rabbit me, but I'd rather ride forty miles after a fox!"

"Where are your fellow-travellers? Are they fairly housed?"

"I should think so. They have been led wildly astray, and there's not a pond or slough within five miles but they can tell the taste of."

"Ha! I understand,—you led them in a round, and have brought them home again?"

"Just so: they are at this minute fairly lodged in the horse-pond at the bottom of the garden."

"But no accident, I hope?"

"No, no; only mother is confoundedly frightened. She thinks herself forty miles off. Now, if your own horses are ready, you may whip off with cousin; and there's not a horse on the place fit to follow you."

Hastings, after warmly expressing his thanks, hastened away, just as Mrs. Hardcastle entered, much bedraggled and sadly frightened. Her fright was redoubled when her graceless son told her that they were upon Crackskull Common, a noted place for highwaymen. The young rascal took a malicious pleasure in adding to her alarm, affecting to mistake a tree for a horse, and a moving cow for a highwayman with a black hat.

As it happened, however, the trickster quickly found himself in a quandary, for Mr. Hardcastle at that moment approached, taking his evening tour of inspection through his garden. Tony, seeing him at a distance, hastily induced his mother to hide in the bushes, engaging himself to face the highwayman,—"an ill-looking fellow, with pistols as long as my arm."

By the time she was fairly hidden, Mr. Hardcastle came up, and questioned Tony how he had got back so soon, and whom he had been talking to. He protested that there was no one but himself; but the suspicious old gentleman insisted on an investigation. Their prolonged talk had by this time so thoroughly alarmed Mrs. Hardcastle for her darling son that she now ran forward, exclaiming,—

"Take my money—my life—good gentleman! Whet your rage on me ; but spare my darling son, if you have any mercy!"

"My wife! as I am a Christian!" exclaimed Mr. Hardcastle.

"Take compassion on us, good Mr. Highwayman!" she implored, kneeling. "Take all our money, but spare our lives! We will never bring you to justice, indeed we won't!"

"Why, Dorothy, woman, are you out of your senses?"

"Mr. Hardcastle, as I'm alive!" cried the good lady. "My fears blinded me. But what has brought you to follow us to this frightful place, so far from home?"

"So far from home! Why, Dorothy, you are not forty yards from your own door. This is one of your old tricks, you graceless rogue!" he said, sharply to Tony. "Don't you remember the horse-pond, my dear?"

"I shall remember it as long as I live," she answered, with a sudden grasp of the situation. "And it is to you, you graceless varlet, I owe all this?"

"Ecod, mother, all the parish says you have spoiled me, and so you may take the fruits on't."

"I'll spoil you, I will," she screamed, flying at him in such a rage that he ran hastily from the spot.

"There's morality, however, in his reply," said Mr. Hardcastle, as he followed at a more sober pace.

Meanwhile Hastings had rescued Miss Neville from her difficult situation, and was earnestly seeking to persuade her to consent to the elopement. He found an unexpected obstacle. She was too much shaken by her adventure to be equal, just then, for any new one, and somewhat remorseful besides. She, therefore, expressed herself as determined to give up the scheme and trust to Mr. Hardcastle's aid for redress.

"He cannot relieve you though he wished to," pleaded her lover. "He has no power in your case."

"But he has influence, and on that I am resolved to rely."

"I have no hopes," answered Hastings. "But since you persist, I must reluctantly obey you."

While the fortunes of Hastings and his lady-love were advancing to this critical stage, other interesting events were occurring in the Hard-castle mansion. Kate had duly told her father of young Marlow's belief that the house was an inn, greatly to the old gentleman's amusement, who saw at once the explanation of his guest's seeming impertinence. While he was still laughing heartily at this discovery, Sir Charles Marlow arrived, and on hearing from Mr. Hardcastle the story of the ridiculous mistake, joined with him to the full in his mirth.

The day's mistakes, however, were not yet at an end. Marlow had not discovered that Miss Hardcastle and the supposed bar-maid were one and the same, and he still stood in awe and terror of the fine lady with whom he had held such a distracting interview. Mr. Hardcastle, on the contrary, with good reason believed that intimate relations existed between the young man and his daughter, having seen him seize her hand and attempt to steal a kiss from her lips.

"Nothing has passed between us but the most profound respect on my side, and the most distant reserve on hers," Marlow protested. "We had but one interview, and that was formal, modest, and uninteresting."

"Well, well, I like modesty in its place well enough," said Mr. Hardcastle to himself, "but this fellow's formal, modest impudence is beyond bearing."

"What am I to think of these two stories?" asked Sir Charles, after his son had left the room. "I dare pledge my honor on his truth."

"And I my happiness on Kate's veracity."

Kate entered the room during their conversation, and was eagerly questioned on the subject in debate. She astounded Sir Charles by protesting that she had had several interviews with his son, and that he had made love to her in anything but a formal fashion. Sir Charles found this difficult to credit. That his backward son could have so utterly changed his character,—it was beyond belief.

"I will convince you to your face of my sincerity," said Miss Hardcastle. "If you and papa will place yourselves behind that screen, you shall hear him declare his passion to me as ardently as you could wish."

This was an easy method of settling the difficulty. The two fathers hid themselves behind the screen just as Marlow returned to the room. On seeing Miss Hardcastle alone he renewed his ardent demonstrations, declaring that he must leave the house, but that it almost broke his heart to part with her. In the end his ardor grew so great that he fell on his knees, and, grasping her hand, vowed himself ready to give up everything in return for her affection, for she had won a heart that hitherto had been closed to love.

This was more than his father could bear. He broke from his ambush, crying out loudly, "I can stand this no longer! Charles, Charles, how have you deceived me? Is this your formal and uninteresting conversation?"

"Your cold reserve?" added Mr. Hardcastle. "What have you to say now, young man?"

"That I am all amazement. What can it mean?"

"That you can address a lady in private and deny it in public. That you have one story for us, and another for my daughter."

"Daughter!—this lady your daughter?"

"Yes, sir, my only daughter; my Kate."

"Oh!" cried Marlow, desperately.

"Yes, sir," laughed Kate, "that identical tall, squinting lady you were pleased to take me for.

She that you addressed as the mild, modest, sentimental man of gravity, and the bold, forward, agreeable Rattle of the ladies' club; ha! ha! ha!"

This completed Marlow's defeat. He turned to fly, but was prevented by Mr. Hardcastle.

"By my hand, you shall not. I see how it is, —all a mistake, and my sly Kate at the bottom of it. Take courage, man, we all forgive you. Won't you forgive him, Kate?"

Kate had little time to answer, for Mrs. Hardcastle now came into the room in a hot fluster,—followed by her son Tony. "They are gone," she cried; "but let them go, I care not. Her fortune is in my hands, and shall remain there."

"Who are gone?" asked her husband.

"My dutiful niece and her gentleman, Mr. Hastings."

"My honest George Hastings?" exclaimed Sir Charles. "The girl could not have made a better choice; there is no worthier fellow living."

"As for her fortune," said Mr. Hardcastle, "you know it is hers, if your son, when of age, refuses to marry her."

"But he is not of age, and she has not waited for his refusal."

She turned as she spoke, and was astonished to see the supposed runaways before her. They had just entered the room.

"We have thought better of it," said Hastings; "and have come back to beg pardon for our rash intention."

"I'm glad to see you back. This may be settled in an easier way," said Mr. Hardcastle. "Come hither, Tony. Do you refuse this lady's hand?"

"I can't refuse her till I'm of age, father."

"Which you are. Your mother and I have kept your age secret, to see if you would mend your ways. But since she puts it to a wrong use, I must declare that you have been of age these three months."

"Hurrah! Then this is the first use I shall make of my liberty." He took Miss Neville's hand. "Witness all men by these presents that I, Anthony Lumpkin, Esquire, of Blank Place, refuse you, Constantia Neville, spinster, of no place at all, for my true and lawful wife. So you can marry whom you please, and Tony Lumpkin is his own man again!"

"My undutiful offspring!" groaned Mrs. Hardcastle.

"Joy, my dear George," exclaimed Marlow. "Now, if I can prevail upon my tyrant here to forgive me for loving her as a bar-maid, and accept me as a lady, I shall be the happiest man alive."

"Why, if so little will make you happy——" began Kate.

"If she makes you as good a wife as she has me a daughter, you will never repent of your bargain," broke in Mr. Hardcastle. "Take her, and with her my blessing; and as you have been so happily mistaken in the mistress, my wish is, that you may never be mistaken in the wife."

THE ROAD TO RUIN.

BY THOMAS HOLCROFT.

[THE author of the above-named play was born at London in 1745. His father was by turns horse-dealer, shoemaker, and peddler; and the son, after three years' apprenticeship as a stable-boy, became successively shoemaker, school-master, and private secretary, and began his dramatic life in 1770 as a strolling player. In this profession he had not much success, and gradually devoted himself to authorship, "Alwyn," the first of his four novels, being published in 1780; and "Duplicity," the first of more than thirty plays, in 1781. He also made good translations of numerous French and German works.

The most successful of his plays was the "Road to Ruin," which brought him large financial returns, and is still classed among acting comedies. In his later life Holcroft met with various troubles. Being an ardent democrat, he was indicted, in 1794, for high treason, with Horne Tooke and others. These proceedings fell through, but party animosity injured the success of his plays, and he became much reduced in means. He died in 1809.]

Harry Dornton, junior member of the firm of Dornton & Co., bankers, of London, had long pursued a course of life that threatened to bring ruin on himself and bankruptcy on the wealthy banking-house to which he was allied. Led into extravagance by the foolish indulgence of his doting father, he had of late years grown notorious for the boldness of his gambling operations and the amount of his losses; there was not a sporting match in the city free from his reckless bets, not a race without his wager on some doubtful horse, while his ordinary associates were a crew of knaves, blacklegs, and *débauchées*,—human pitch which no one could touch without being defiled.

These excesses had at length driven his father to desperation. He loved his son as warmly as ever, but was goaded almost to madness by his vices, and in the end ordered that his name should be stricken from the firm, and no more drafts of his be honored. He went even further than this. Furious at his son's not having returned home at two o'clock in the morning, until which hour he had awaited him, he gave orders to the servants to lock up the house and go to bed, threatening to discharge any one who should admit the profligate.

"It's all ended," he declared to his cashier. "Observe, not a guinea to the spendthrift. If you lend him any yourself, I'll not pay you. I'll no longer be a fond, doting father. Take warning, I say. Though you should hereafter see him begging, starving in the streets, not so much as the loan or the gift of a single guinea."

"I shall be careful to obey your orders, sir."

"What! would you see him starve and not lend him a guinea?" exclaimed the father, with a sudden change of feeling. "Could you, sir?"

"Certainly not; except in obedience to your orders."

"Could any orders justify your seeing an unfortunate youth, rejected by his father, abandoned by his friends, starving to death?"

Thus the fond old man went on, vacillating between anger at his son's vices and affection for his person, till the distracted servants knew not what to do. This conversation ended with the appearance of his partner, Mr. Sulky, who showed the angry banker a newspaper paragraph that added new fuel to his indignation. The disheartening story it told was that the profligate youth had lost the large sum of ten thousand pounds at the Newmarket races.

"What proof have you of this?" exclaimed Mr. Dornton, trembling with emotion. "It must be a lie!"

"Bills at three days' sight, for the full amount, have already been presented."

"And accepted?"

"Yes."

"But—why—were you mad, Mr. Sulky? Were you mad, sir?"

"I soon shall be."

"The credit of my house is beginning to totter. What will, what must be the effect of such a paragraph?"

"I can tell you, sir. A run against the house, stoppage, disgrace, bankruptcy."

These words, and the fatal picture they presented to Mr. Dornton's imagination, stirred his anger to frenzy. He bade Mr. Smith, the cashier, to call the servants together, and forbid them under penalty of instant dismissal, to let their young master set foot in the house. As for himself, he ordered them to fetch his blunderbuss, and loaded it to the muzzle, wildly vowing to riddle the young scoundrel with bullets if he should have the effrontery to appear.

While this exciting scene was going on within the house, Harry Dornton, with his sporting associate, Jack Milford, was approaching the outside at the speed of a pair of smoking horses. Springing from the post-chaise, and dismissing the postilions, the young profligate advanced to the door, and knocked loudly for admittance.

The only effect of his summons was the furious throwing up of a window over his head, and the appearance of his father with a blunderbuss, threatening to fill him with bullets if he dared to knock again.

"So! dad is in his tantrums again!" was the remark of the young hopeful.

"You have given him some cause," answered

Milford. "We shall not get in." While these words were being spoken, Mr. Sulky had appeared at the window and drawn Mr. Dornton away, shutting down the sash.

"Not get in!" answered Harry. "Little you know my father. The door will open in less than fifteen seconds."

"Done, for a hundred!"

"Done, done!" They took out their watches, but at this instant the door opened. "I have you, Jack; double or quits we find the cloth laid, and supper on the table."

"No, no, that won't do."

Despite their bravado, however, it was not a very agreeable situation in which the two gamesters found themselves. Mr. Dornton, filled with rage at the disobedience to his orders, instantly discharged the servant who had let Harry in; a sentence which Harry negatived, as soon as he heard of it, by telling the fellow to return to his duties.

While the young men stood debating the situation, Mr. Sulky entered, and in his short, curt manner took Harry severely to task, telling him that, not content with ruining himself, he had at last succeeded in ruining his father, whose great wealth had been so reduced by the past five years of profligacy that bankruptcy now stared him in the face.

Having thus delivered himself to Harry, he turned to Milford, and sternly charged him with having ruined, by his evil counsels, the son of the generous man who had loaned him five thousand pounds.

"Ruined me!" cried Harry. "Don't believe a word of that, my good grumbler; I ruined myself; I needed no guide on the road to ruin."

"As for me," said Milford, "my father died immensely rich. Though I may be what the law calls illegitimate, yet I ought not to starve. You, who are my father's executor, should be the last to blame me, and should prevail on the Widow Warren to do me justice."

It is necessary, at this point, to tell something further concerning the history of young Milford, that the reader may the better comprehend what is to follow. He, as he had himself said, was the illegitimate son of a wealthy alderman named Warren, who a few years before had married a middle-aged widow, with a daughter, Sophia, by her first husband.

Six months before the opening of our story the alderman had died, leaving Mr. Sulky the executor of his will. But his death took place in the south of France, and the will had completely disappeared. He had either hid it too carefully, or had given it into the care of some unfaithful custodian. The Widow Warren had, in consequence, come into full possession of the property, and refused to help with a penny the son whom there was good reason to believe had been made his father's heir.

What Mr. Sulky now proceeded to say was of the greatest interest to the unlucky son. He stated that he had just received a letter informing him that the will had been found, locked in a private drawer, and that a month before it had been intrusted to a gentleman of Montpellier, who was coming to England.

So far all seemed promising, but Mr. Sulky concluded by saying that no such gentleman had called upon him, and that he strongly suspected that the will had somehow fallen into the widow's hands.

"You are a couple of pretty gentlemen," he finished. "But beware; misfortune is at your heels. Mr. Dornton vows vengeance on you both, and justly. He is not gone to bed, and if you have confidence to look him in the face, stay where you are."

"I neither wish to insult nor be insulted," said Milford," and will not wait Mr. Dornton's appearance." He turned on his heel with these words, and left the house.

He had but fairly gone when Mr. Dornton entered, white with anger, and holding in his hand the paper which contained the statement of his son's latest disgraceful performance. Harry found himself assailed with a volley of abuse, in which "scoundrel" was one of the mildest terms. His father told him that he had erased his name from the list of members of the firm, and ended by passionately exclaiming,—

"If I should happily outlive the storm you have raised, it shall not be to support a prodigal, or to reward a gambler. You are disinherited. I'll no longer act the doting father, fascinated by your arts."

"I never had any art, sir, except the one you taught me," answered Harry, mildly.

"I taught you! What, scoundrel? What?"

"That of loving you, sir."

"Loving me!"

"Most sincerely."

"Why, can you say, Harry,—rascal, I mean,—that you love me?"

"I should be a rascal, indeed, if I did not, sir."

"Harry, Harry!" cried the old gentleman, in great agitation. "No, confound me if I do! Sir, you are a vile——"

"I know I am."

"And I'll never speak to you again."

"Dear father, reproach me with my follies, dismiss me from the firm, disinherit me. I deserve it all, and more. But say, 'good-night, Harry.'"

"I won't! I won't!" exclaimed Mr. Dornton, as he ran furiously from the room.

"Say you so. Why, then, my noble-hearted dad, I am indeed a scoundrel!"

"Good-night," cried Mr. Dornton, at this moment, showing his agitated face at the door.

"Good-night," answered Harry, his face lighting up with a warm expression, while his heart swelled with an earnest resolution of reform.

It is now our duty to introduce to the reader another important personage of our story, the Widow Warren. This relict of two husbands was a silly old fool, who dressed like a girl, put on the vainest airs, and set herself ardently to the catching of a third husband,—one of the chief lures to which was the money of the late alderman, which she held with the greed of miser.

This coquette of forty summers fancied in her silly soul that Harry Dornton was in love with her youthful charms. He came, indeed, often to her house, but the real attraction was her daughter Sophia, a hoidenish girl of eighteen, who had been brought up in the country with the notions and feelings of a child, but was as generous at heart as her mother was miserly.

Mr. Sulky, who in spite of his brusque manners and show of surliness, was full of the milk of human kindness, called on the widow on the day after the scene just described, with the hope of inducing her to do justice to the son of her late husband. He found his mission in vain. The woman hid her coldness of heart behind her frivolity, and the graff messenger at length gave up his mission in disgust, finding that he could get her to talk of nothing but her lovers.

"Whom will you make love to next, woman?" he snarled. "Even I am not secure in your company."'

"Love to you? Ha! ha! ha! You carica-
ture of tenderness! But if you *should* happen
to see Mr. Dornton, do a good-natured thing for
once, and tell him I'm at home all day."

With these words she mincingly left the room,
with an affected air of youthfulness, leaving her
visitor to make his way out as he pleased. He
had barely gone when Harry Dornton himself
appeared. A servant, with a handful of bills, followed him into the house.

"What are all these?" asked the young profligate.

"Tradesmen's bills, sir. They came this morning, and Mr. Smith sent me after you with them."

"The deuce! Ill news travels fast, it seems.
Take them all back, and bid my creditors come
themselves to-day. Has Mr. Williams, the hosier,
sent in his bill?"

"No, sir."

"I thought as much; he is the only honest fish
in a shoal of sharks. Tell him to come with the
rest, and, on his life, not to fail."

"Very well, sir."

The departure of the servant was followed by
the entrance of Sophia, who had been apprised
of her lover's visit. She was dressed like a girl
of fifteen, and had the overflowing spirits of a
hoidenish country girl; informing Harry that
she could not think of loving him, however he
might plead, for her grandma had told her it
would be a sin to love till she was one-and-twenty;

that Valentine's day was five weeks gone, and nobody had sent her a valentine; that if she were to find such a thing under her pillow, or baked in a plum-cake, she—— and so on in a flood of childish tattle.

This interesting love-scene was interrupted by the entrance of Goldfinch, a wild young reprobate, who was one of Harry's sporting companions, and of Mrs. Warren's coterie of lovers; and of Jack Milford, who was on his way to the tennis court, where a great match was to be played.

Harry refused to accompany him. He was done with all that, he said, and would never bet another guinea. Yet five minutes of Milford's laughing solicitations were enough to overcome his good resolutions, and the three gamesters were quickly off to the scene of sport. Jack, however, had achieved an unlucky success for himself. Mr. Dornton, who blamed him as the leading agent in his son's excesses, had sued out a writ against him for one thousand pounds, and stationed a sheriff's officer at the door of the tennis court, with orders to arrest him if he should bring his son thither.

The arrest was duly made. Milford sent word to Harry, who had passed on into the court, that he was in trouble; but the young gambler, in whom the passion for betting was now fully aroused, sent word back that he would not leave the court for a thousand pounds; so the spendthrift was borne off to prison, though he pitifully begged for but five minutes to see the game.

While the young gamester was thus paying the penalty of his reckless course, events were happening of far more moment to him than an arrest for debt. In short, the large estate left by his father was on the point of slipping from his hands to the unyielding grip of the Widow Warren. An unlucky complication of events had arisen, through the fact that there was a note-broker in London of the name of Silky,—a smooth rogue, as soft as silk without and as hard as stone within. The Spanish gentleman who brought Mr. Warren's will to London made a mistake of names, and carried it to Mr. Silky instead of to Mr. Sulky, the true executor. Before the mistake could be corrected this gentleman was taken very ill at his hotel, and died there after a short sickness.

News of his death was not long in reaching Mr. Silky, in whose greedy soul a plot to cheat the real heir and benefit himself was quickly devised. Jack Milford's heirship under the will depended upon a certain contingency. If the widow should marry, the property ceased to be hers, and it was the rascal's design, by threatening to make public the will, to induce her to marry some gentleman of easy conscience, who would be willing to pay roundly for the prize of a rich bride.

For this purpose he settled on Goldfinch, who had already run through his patrimony, and was one of the widow's most ardent suitors. The plotting villain sent for this wild spendthrift, and told him that the late alderman had left not less than one hundred and fifty thousand pounds, that he had a hold on the widow, and could make her marry whom he pleased, and that his price for the sale of her hand was fifty thousand pounds,—not a penny less. Goldfinch, who would have sold his soul for money to bet on horses, readily agreed, and Silky told him that he must get Mrs. Warren's written promise to the marriage, with a good round penalty in case of forfeiture,—not less than twenty thousand pounds. In that case the confederates were to divide. To this part of the plot Goldfinch agreed as readily as to the other, and all seemed promising for the success of Mr. Silky's scheme.

The conspirators were not long in putting their precious scheme in execution, but they found an obstacle in an unexpected quarter,—the widow herself. Mr. Silky called on her without delay, and showed her the will, from which he read the following significant clause:

"But as I have sometimes painfully suspected the excessive affection which my said wife, Winifred Warren, professed for me during my decline, and that the solemn protestations which she made never to marry again, should she survive me, were done with sinister views, it is my will that, should she marry or give a legal promise of marriage, written or verbal, she shall be cut off with an annuity of six hundred a year; the residue of my effects in that case to be equally divided between my natural son, John Milford, and my wife's daughter, Sophia Freelove."

"Six hundred a year! The old dotard! brute! monster!" broke out the widow in a rage. "I hate him now as heartily as when he was alive! But pray, sir, how came you by this will?"

This the cunning Mr. Silky made no hesitation in telling her, and also in informing her that he was ready to help her to a husband in spite of the will, no less a person than the handsome and well-born Mr. Goldfinch, whom she could have for the small gratuity of fifty thousand pounds.

"You are a shocking old miser, Mr. Silky," answered the widow. "But I have made a conquest that places me beyond your power. I mean to marry Mr. Dornton."

"What! old Mr. Dornton, madam?"

"No, sir; the gay and gallant young Mr. Dornton, the lawful monarch of my bleeding heart."

"Young Mr. Dornton!" echoed the broker, with a laugh of high amusement.

"Yes, sir; so you may take your will and light your fires with it. Mr. Sulky, the executor, is Mr. Dornton's partner, and when I marry Mr. Dornton, he will never inflict the absurd penalty."

"Very true, madam; he certainly never will,—when you marry Mr. Dornton."

Mr. Silky returned home, bursting into little peals of satirical laughter as he went along the street. The idea of the elegant Harry Dornton marrying this ill-preserved old widow seemed to him so supremely ridiculous that he felt not the shadow of a doubt as to the success of his neatly-laid matrimonial scheme.

Unluckily for him, however, circumstances were arising which were likely to prove disastrous to his plots, and his own greed and ingratitude were destined to play a vital part in this chain of events. They began in the disaster which Mr. Sulky had anticipated, but which Harry Dornton had laughed to scorn, a run on the banking house of Dornton & Co. The news published the day before, of the young spendthrift's heavy losses at the Newcastle races, had so alarmed the creditors of the bank that at the hour of opening they came in throngs to present their bills; and in spite of every device to protract payment, money was drawn from the Dornton coffers with perilous rapidity.

Among these creditors were the tradesmen whom Harry had bidden to present their bills for payment; a set of sharks who, through his heedlessness as to his purchases, had charged him threefold for everything he bought. The only honest one among them was the hosier, on whose presence Harry had insisted, and who begged to let his bill stand, telling Mr. Dornton that Harry had saved him and his family from ruin.

"You are an honest fellow," cried Mr. Dornton, warmly shaking his hand. "And so Harry has been your friend? Come, I'll pay this bill myself."

While the worthy banker was telling the others that he would have nothing to do with their bills, Harry entered, and on him the old gentleman emptied the vials of his accumulating wrath.

" I know my faults, and am ready to pay their penalty," said Harry, earnestly. "But, sir, you have paid my debts of honor, do not let my tradesmen go unpaid. The whole is but five thousand pounds."

"*But* five thousand! Why, sirrah, you have loaded our counters with ruin!"

"No, no,—I have been a sad scapegrace, I know; but not even my extravagance can shake this house."

The confident fellow was destined to become quickly better informed. As they stood talking, Mr. Smith, the cashier, rushed in, and exclaimed, in consternation, that at the rate bills were being presented the bank could not long meet its demands. Harry gazed at him with a consternation equal to his own.

" Are you serious?" he asked.

" Sir?"

" Are you serious, I say? Is not this some trick to impose on me?"

"Look into the shop, sir, and convince yourself," answered the cashier. " If we do not have a supply within an hour, we must stop payment."

"My father disgraced and ruined! Is it possible?" exclaimed Harry, wildly. "And by me? Are these things so?"

"Harry, how you look! You frighten me!" cried the anxious father.

"Ruined by me? It shall be done! Don't despair, my dear, good, wronged father! I'll find relief."

"Harry! Harry! Where would you go? What would you do? Oh, stay!"

"I'll not be long. I brought this ruin on you. I'll retrieve it, if I sacrifice myself tenfold."

He rushed into the street with these words, in a state of desperation that left his father so overwhelmed with anxiety and fear as nearly to forget the impending disaster to his fortune.

The excited youth had two plans in his distracted mind,—one, an appeal to the gratitude of a miser; one, to the love of a woman. The broker, Mr. Silky, rich as he now was, had been, not five years before, on the brink of ruin, from which he had been rescued by the generous aid of Harry Dornton. Harry now called on him and demanded a return of this favor, begging that he would come at once to the aid of the house of Dornton & Co., to the extent of fifty thousand pounds.

The news of the impending failure had not yet reached the ears of Mr. Silky, and at first he freely acknowledged his obligations to his visitor, and the wealth which Harry's timely aid had brought him. But on learning the danger which

overhung the house of Dornton & Co., his tune
changed, and he suddenly grew poor and embarrassed. He would do anything under heaven to
show his gratitude, but,—as to putting his hand in
his pocket,—with the daily demands on him——

In the end the indignant young man, choking
with fury, hurled the miserable creature across
his room, and with a cry of "scoundrel!" rushed
from the house, to keep himself from the tempta-
tion to murder the ungrateful wretch.

From the office of Mr. Silky he made his way
in all haste to the residence of the Widow Warren, now so stung by remorse that he was ready
to make the most degrading sacrifices to save his
father from ruin. On his way thither he stopped
and drank deeply, so that he burst in upon the
old coquette with an aspect of wild gayety that
was due partly to wine, partly to affected passion.

His wooing was begun in an excited manner
that sadly frightened the enamored widow, but
when he called upon her frantically to accept
his hand, she was only too ready to yield to his
wild appeal.

"But," he continued, with a realizing sense of
the situation, "I have ruined my father! To
save him have I fallen in love! I must have
money—money! We'll be married to-night,
widow. But early in the morn, ere counters echo
with the ring of gold, fifty thousand pounds must
be raised."

"It shall, dear Mr. Dornton."

"Remember. The first thing in the morning."

"Why not a part this evening? I have a tri-fling sum,—six thousand,—which I meant to dis-pose of,—but——"

"I'll dispose of it, dear widow!" He kissed her. "Doubt not my gratitude. Let this—and this——" Kissing her again.

"Fie! you sad man. I'll bring a draft. But remember, this trifle is for your own use."

"No,—for my father. Save but my father, and I'll kiss the ground you tread on, my empress of the golden isles!"

Harry's affected love for his over-bloomed be-trothed was to experience an unpleasant inter-ruption. For just as the happy widow returned with the draft, and her tipsy lover kneeled at her feet in gratitude, and caught her hand to kiss it, Sophia entered, and stood aghast at the dis-tracting spectacle.

Then the poor girl burst into tears, vowed she would go down to Gloucestershire, to her dear, dear grandma, and taking from her bosom the valen-tine,—which Harry had sent her that morning baked in a plum cake,—tore it to pieces and flung the fragments at his feet.

"Widow, I'm a vile fellow; don't have me!" cried Harry. "You are right to despise me, Sophy. I've sold myself, and six thousand pounds is the money paid down. But I love you, Sophy."

"You are a base, faithless man!" cried the girl.

"And you are a pitiless woman, if you are my

mother, to let my brother Milford lie in a dark dungeon!"

"What! Milford in prison?"

"Yes, sir; arrested by your cruel, old, ugly father!"

"Is this true, widow?" asked Harry.

"Sir——" she stammered.

"Arrested by my father? And you, squandering your money on a ruined reprobate, yet refuse to release your husband's son?"

"Nay, but, dear Mr. Dornton——"

"That will do, widow. You'll see me again soon," and Harry rushed from the house, nearly sobered by indignation.

The half-maddened youth hurried to the residence of the sheriff's officer, in which he had learned that his friend was detained, and ordered the officer to write an acquittal instantly for the thousand pounds, for which he was held.

"A thousand, sir! it is almost five thousand now," answered the officer, "retainers have been lodged for that amount."

"Five thousand?"

"Must I write an acquittal for that sum?"

"No,—yes, write it; have it ready. It shall be paid to-morrow morning."

"In the mean time, there may be more retainers."

"The devil! What shall I do? Let me see him. Send him here; but not a word, mind you. Send a bottle of champagne and two rummers."

It had been better if Harry had not seen his friend, for he found him coldly indignant, refusing to drink, and in the end angrily declaring that he had been betrayed by him and imprisoned by his father, and all to get him out of the way, that he might prosecute his designs on Mrs. Warren without interruption.

This assault took Harry sadly aback; but his surprise became indignation when Milford accused his father of meanness and malice.

"Think what you will of me," he exclaimed; "but not a word against my father!"

"He is pitifully malignant," persisted Milford. "Not content with the little vengeance he could take himself, he has sent word round to all my creditors."

"It is a vile falsehood!" cried Harry, in a passion. "Mr. Milford, you shall hear from me immediately," and he left the room full of indignation.

In a few minutes afterwards the sheriff's officer entered, and gave Milford a note, which he said came from the young gentleman who had just left him.

"I understand you are at liberty," the note ran. "I shall walk up to Hyde Park, where we can settle this little dispute. You will find me at the ring at six. Exactly at six."

"At liberty! What does he mean?" Milford looked at the officer.

"Your debts are all discharged, sir."

" Discharged?   By whom ?"

" Why, sir—that is——"

" Tell me the truth at once."

" I perceive, sir, there has been some warmth
between you and the young gentleman; and
though he made me promise silence and secrecy——"

" What! then it was Mr. Dornton ?" The officer
bowed. "Madman, what have I done ?" and Milford rushed from the room in a passion of
remorse.

The tidings of Harry Dornton's wooing of
the Widow Warren, a rumor of which had so
quickly reached the ears of his friend Milford,
was not much longer in reaching the banking-
house of his father. Harry had gone there after
his quarrel with Milford, and, finding that the
run still continued, his agony of conscience grew
so great that he confessed to Mr. Smith what he
intended to do for his father's relief, and hurried
out in a fever of distress.

Mr. Smith hastened to repeat the story to Mr.
Dornton, telling him that Harry had already received six thousand pounds from his intended
bride. The distraction of the old man reached
its climax at this unwelcome news. His son
marry that woman? He would die himself first!
The money must be repaid.

" What bank have we to begin with to-morrow ?" he asked of Mr. Sulky, when the latter
entered, from his strenuous efforts to raise funds.

"I can't tell; I fear not thirty thousand."

"Six thousand, then, is a great sum. But do you think I ought not to venture?"

"Venture what?"

"To—to take it from our bank."

"For what?"

"For—for the—the relief of Harry Dornton!"

"Take all!" exclaimed Mr. Sulky, in a rage. "What is it to me? I can stare bankruptcy in the face as steadfastly as you can."

"I see. The world is all alike. I am an old fool, and so shall live and die."

"Why do you ask my advice? Take the money! Empty the coffers! Pour it all into his hat! Give him guineas to play at chuck-farthing, and bank bills to curl his hair!"

"So, Mr. Sulky, you would see him married to this widow, to whom you have often given the worst of characters, rather than incur a little more risk for your friend?"

"Marry? Marry whom?"

"The Widow Warren, I tell you."

"Harry Dornton?"

"Yes, Harry Dornton."

"When? Where?"

"Immediately. With unexampled affection, he is about to sacrifice his youth and hopes of happiness in order to save me from ruin with this woman's money."

"Marry her?—Take the money! Away! I

would starve inchmeal rather than he should marry that cormorant!"

"Mr. Sulky, you are a worthy man, a true friend."

"Curse compliments, make haste!"

Make haste he did, for not half an hour had elapsed from his son's departure before he appeared at the widow's house, prepared to repay the money which she had advanced.

He found affairs there in a somewhat distracted state. Sophia was half wild between her sense of the treachery of her lover, the folly of her mother, and her belief that her heart's affection was to be sacrificed. The widow, on the other hand, was so filled with vanity and conceit that she put on the airs of a peacock, and dressed herself with girlish ribands and ringlets dangling down her back. When Mr. Dornton appeared, Mrs. Warren, who hand never before seen him, fancied him to be the parson whom his son had promised to send.

A conversation ensued that was marked by ridiculous cross-conceptions, the two falling into a snarl of misunderstandings which only by the appearance of Harry and his addressing the supposed clergyman as his father were able to overcome. The widow had expressed an unflattering opinion of Mr. Dornton, senior, to the supposed clergyman, and was covered with confusion on learning with whom she had been speaking.

"Never retract, madam," remarked Mr. Dornton. "Let us continue the like plain, honest dealing. As for you, Harry, this absurd match is at an end. I am come to say that our danger is over."

"Over? Are you serious, sir?"

"Yes. Our books have been examined, and show a far better condition than we hoped; and Mr. Sulky's rich uncle has died and left him sole heir. As for you, madam, here is your money."

"Nay, but—Mr. Dornton—sir——" And the widow burst into tears, "I don't want the filthy money. And as to what I said, though you have arrested Mr. Milford——"

"Ha!" exclaimed Harry, suddenly changing from his aspect of joy to one of anxiety. He looked at his watch. There was barely time to keep his appointment with Jack Milford. He hastened to the door.

"Where are you going, Harry?" cried his father. "Come back, sir! Stay, I say!"

"I cannot stay. My honor is at stake." And he hastily fled from the room.

"His honor! Here, madam, take your money. His honor at stake!" Flinging the draft on the table, Mr. Dornton hurried away in pursuit of his impulsive son.

"Cruel usage! Faithless, blind, stupid men!" exclaimed the weeping widow. "I'll forsake and forswear the whole sex."

Mrs. Warren was not quite in earnest in this.

In the midst of her tears Mr. Goldfinch made his appearance, and pressed his suit with such vigor that the disappointed woman, deeming that she had better catch a gudgeon than no fish at all, permitted him to "tyrannize over her palpitating heart," as she expressed it, and agreed to write and sign a promise to that effect.

Unfortunately for her plans, she had chosen a fool for a husband, a youth who was quite willing to sell himself for money, but had not the wit to hold his tongue. In fact, he revealed her secret to the very person of all from whom it was her best interest to conceal it,—to Jack Milford, who entered the room after she had retired to draw up the promise of marriage.

In his wild flow of spirits Goldfinch told his friend that he had captured the widow, and was off post-haste for old Mr. Silky.

"Silky, did you say?"

"Yes. I'm to pay the miserly rascal fifty thousand down. Mum; it's a secret; but he has her; she can't marry without his consent."

"Why?"

"Don't know. He has got some deed,—some writing. The close old rogue won't tell. Good-by, Jack. I'll make the horses fly faster than ever. Wait till I finger the widow's ducats. Good-by." And off he fled, after having done his utmost to ruin his hopes and the widow's plans.

"Fifty thousand to Silky for his consent! Because of some writing! Can it be the will? It must! By heaven, it must!" And Milford left the room in as great haste as Goldfinch had done.

While Milford had been speeding to Mrs. Warren's house, in hopes to see and thank Harry for his timely aid, the latter was making all haste to Hyde Park, to keep his duelling appointment; while his father was following him with equal haste. Father and son reached the appointed place almost together.

"What do you here, Harry?" asked Mr. Dornton, severely.

"Sir, I—I want air."

"And I want information. What brought you hither? Where's the money you had of the widow?"

"Gone, sir. Most of it."

"Gone! And your creditors not paid!"

"No, sir."

"I suspected—I foreboded this," exclaimed the distracted father, wringing his hands. "He has been at some gaming house, lost all, quarrelled, and come here to put a miserable end to a miserable existence. Oh, who would be a father!"

The saddened old gentleman was interrupted by a messenger, who came in and handed him a note. "From Mr. Milford, sir."

"It is for me, then," said Harry.

"That is to be seen," rejoined his father, shortly. "This is no time for ceremony." He tore it open and read it. "'Dear Harry, forgive the provocation I have given you; forgive the wrongs I have done your father. I will submit to any disgrace rather than lift my hand against your life. I would have come and apologized even on my knees, but am prevented. J. MILFORD.'"

"Harry, what means this?" exclaimed the old man, with a change of expression. "Tell me, is it in paying Milford's debts that you have expended that money?"

"It is, sir."

"But why did you come here to fight him?"

"Sir, he—he spoke disrespectfully of you."

"Harry!" cried Mr. Dornton, looking on him with strong emotion, and then suddenly seizing his hand. "Harry! Do with me what you will! Oh, who would not be a father!"

"Dear sir, let us fly to console poor Milford."

Poor Milford was just then doing his best to console himself. He had hastened from Mrs. Warren's mansion to the Dornton banking-house, got possession of Mr. Sulky, and brought him back in all haste, telling him by the way of the valuable secret he had discovered.

"They mean to destroy the will," he said, on entering the room at the widow's which he had recently left. "Goldfinch is just returned with Silky. No doubt they will be here immediately to settle the business in private. Here are two closets,—do you hide in one, and I will in the other. We can hear what they are about, and burst out on them at the proper moment."

"I hate hiding. It's deceit, and deceit is the resource of a rascal."

"There is no help for it. It is too late to get legal assistance. I hear them coming. Make haste!"

"Well, if it must be so."

· They had hardly disappeared in the closets when Silky, Goldfinch, and Mrs. Warren entered the room in company. Deeming themselves safe from interruption, they talked with freedom of their purposes, Mr. Silky telling his companions that he did not wish to delay their matrimonial purposes, but first needed their signatures to a legal instrument, which he had prepared for his own security.

To make all safe, however, the cautious villain first locked the two doors of the room, and then, for double assurance, locked the closet doors also. This done, they prepared to go through with the business of signing. But they were interrupted in the midst of their operations by a distracting incident,—a knock from within one of the closets. They started back from the table in alarm ; which was redoubled the minute afterwards by as loud a knock from the other closet.

"The candles burn blue!" exclaimed Silky.

"Nonsense, it's only cats in the closets," answered Goldfinch, recovering from his fright. "Come, I'll sign."

He signed the bond, an action in which he was followed by the widow.

"Well done," said Silky. "Here, now, is the will. That all may be safe we'll commit it immediately to the flames."

He was about to hold it to the light of the candle when from each closet came two thundering knocks, which so scared him that he dropped one candle and overturned the other.

"Lord have mercy on us!" he cried.

"My hair stands on end!" exclaimed Goldfinch.

"Save me, Mr. Goldfinch!" screamed the widow, as the knocks began again not only in the closets, but at both chamber-doors. "Protect me! Ah!"

She shrieked with terror as both closet-doors were burst open, and two persons sprang into the darkened room, who rushed forward and seized the bond and promise of marriage on the table. They then unlocked the chamber-doors, admitting at once a servant with lights, and at the other Harry and his father, with Sophia.

"Where is the will?" exclaimed Sulky. "Give it to me, you old scoundrel! Give it up this instant, or I'll throttle you!" He grappled the hoary villain, and wrested it from him.

"What has happened, gentlemen?" asked Harry. "How came you thus all locked up together?"

Not many words were needed to explain the highly interesting situation.

"And now, madam——" said Mr. Sulky.

"Keep off, monster!" exclaimed the widow. "You smell of malice, cruelty, and persecution."

"No, madam; I smell of honesty, a drug you nauseate, but which you must take. I have looked over the will, and find that I have the power. You have signed a promise of marriage, and the money has slipped from your grasp."

"Let me go, I hate the sight of you! Your breast is flint, flint, unfeeling gorgon, and I abominate you!" She left the room in a high rage.

"Nay, you are a kind, good, cross old soul," cried Sophia, "and I am sure you'll forgive my poor ma. We ought all to forget and forgive. Ought we not, Mr. Dornton?"

"Do you hear her, sir?" said Harry, to his father.

"Yes, she has a pure and innocent heart. Take her, Harry, you have my blessing and hopes for your happiness."

"La, Mr. Dornton, how could you——" exclaimed Sophia, as Harry sealed the compact with a kiss.

And so our story ends. Goldfinch was advised by Mr. Dornton to leave off his wild courses and turn to trade, but he scouted all such dull modes of life. As for the detected rogue, Mr. Silky, he skulked from the room, bearing with him the sting of Mr. Sulky's very plainly-expressed opinions. Everybody else, however, was overflowing with joy, for the loss of the banker's fortune had been averted, and the two profligate friends were safely checked in their downward course on "The Road to Ruin."

WILD OATS.

BY JOHN O'KEEFE.

[THE author of the play above named, while
he ~~seems to ranked~~ among the great dramatists,
~~is ranked~~ among the most prolific, since
~~is at to produced~~ more than sixty plays, many
of which ~~became~~ highly popular. These plays
are rather extended farces than true comedies,
and while several of ~~them are~~ classed among
the acting drama, ~~only one strongly appeals~~
~~to the~~ ~~Wild Oats,~~" however, is so
~~special~~ ~~character each~~ ~~term~~
of the ~~theatre-going~~ public, that it is ~~likely long~~
to ~~retain its place in~~ the living drama.

John O'Keefe was of Irish birth, ~~being born at~~
~~Dublin in 1747.~~ His life was actively devoted to
~~dramatic composition, he~~ having produced nearly
fifty plays ~~by the end of the century.~~ In his
fiftieth year ~~he became blind~~ ~~continued his~~
work of authorship, and ~~pathetic~~ stories are told
of the blind old playwright ~~listening~~ behind the
~~scenes~~ for the public verdict ~~on~~ his plays, and
~~anxiously~~ questioning his little ~~as~~ to the temper
of the audience. He was ~~poorly~~ supported in his

11   121

WILD OATS.

BY JOHN O'KEEFE.

[THE author of the play above named, while he cannot be ranked among the great dramatists, certainly belongs among the most prolific, since in all he produced more than sixty plays, many of which became highly popular. These plays are rather extended farces than true comedies, and while several of them are still classed among the acting drama, only one strongly appeals to the public taste. "Wild Oats," however, is so sprightly, and its leading character such a favorite of the theatre-going public, that it is likely long to retain its place in the living drama.

John O'Keefe was of Irish birth, being born at Dublin in 1747. His life was actively devoted to dramatic composition, he having produced nearly fifty plays by the end of the century. In his fiftieth year he became blind, yet continued his work of authorship, and pathetic stories are told of the blind old playwright's waiting behind the scenes for the public verdict on his plays, and eagerly questioning his little son as to the temper of the audience. He was partly supported in his later years by a pension from the crown. He died in 1833.]

Sir George Thunder, a captain in the British navy, had sown his wild oats in his youthful days, and had ever since been reaping the harvest in remorse. Under the false name of Captain Seymour he had, as he supposed, with the connivance of a seaman named John Dory, deceived an innocent young lady, named Amelia, by a false marriage. He had afterwards deserted her and her infant son in the East Indies, and subsequently married again,—a base action which had afterwards given his conscience many a bitter pang. In one respect he was mistaken,—his marriage with Amelia had been a real one. Honest John Dory had deceived his scapegrace of a master, the ceremony having been performed by Amelia's brother, who was then in holy orders. Sir George had since risen in rank in the navy, and had kept John Dory with him as his boatswain, and, in a measure, as his guardian. On one occasion, when the bed-curtains of his cabin had caught fire, John had snatched him from his berth and flung him into the sea,—half drowning him to keep him from being burned. On another, when he found him drinking too deeply in company, he had caught him up in his stalwart arms and carried him home, despite his kicks and curses. Other similar evidences of John's idea of duty might be cited; but withal, the small-sized but stout-hearted baronet loved him like a brother, and would rather have lost his right arm than his faithful boatswain.

Shortly before the date of the opening of our story, Sir George—or Captain Thunder, to give his official title—had reached England. He had hoped to pay an early visit to his son, Harry, who had just completed his studies in the Naval Academy at Portsmouth, but was prevented from doing so by the necessity of pursuing some deserters, who had fled after taking his earnest money. He thereupon sent John Dory to Portsmouth to bring his son, and set out in hot chase after the deserters.

Sir George had another purpose in view. In Hampshire, whither his steps were directed, dwelt his niece, Lady Mary Amaranth Thunder,—or Mary Thunder, as she preferred to call herself, for she had been brought up in the plain tenets of the Quakers. The young lady was rich, handsome, and generous, much of her wealth having been left her by a cousin, the executor of whose will, Ephraim Smooth, a canting hypocrite, dwelt with her, as an unwelcome addition to her household. In Sir George's fancy, this fair Quakeress, despite her plain ways, would make a fitting match for his son, and it was with the design of bringing the cousins together that he had sent John Dory to conduct the young man to Hampshire.

The worthy boatswain failed in his mission.

Harry Thunder had left Portsmouth before he got there. The young truant, in fact, was emulating his father in sowing his wild oats. Seeking London, he had joined a company of strolling actors, taking the stage-name of Dick Buskin. Here he became an intimate friend of a high-minded but light-hearted young actor named Jack Rover. The two friends, after playing together for some time, had left the company through some disagreement, and at the time of Sir George's visit to Hampshire were in the same part of England, on their way to Winchester, where they were booked to play.

Sir George, failing to find the deserters, had visited his niece, where, despite her warm welcome, the freedom of speech of the servants roused the ire of the old sea-dog, accustomed to the respect of manners on shipboard. He roared out his opinion of Ephraim Smooth and the others so plainly, indeed, that Lady Amaranth had much trouble to quiet him.

"Kinsman, be patient," she said, soberly. "These are our ways. But I am glad to greet thee, and will be pleased to welcome my cousin Henry, whom I have not beheld these twelve years."

Harry Thunder was just then nearer than either of them suspected. He was, in fact, on a road in the vicinity of Lady Amaranth's mansion, in company with his servant Midge. Their companion, Jack Rover, had not yet left the inn where they had spent the night. Harry took the opportunity for a private conversation with Midge, whom he told that he had decided to bring his frolics to an end, and seek his father, whom he knew to be somewhere in that locality.

"My three months' runaway has brought me some good," he said to himself. "I have seen something of life, had a precious deal of fun, and made acquaintance with the noblest and pleasantest fellow I ever met. If he would only get over his abominable habit of quotation! Here he comes. It hurts me to have to bid him farewell. I hope he will not find the purse I have hid in his coat-pocket before we part."

As he spoke, Rover came up at a rattling pace, singing a rollicking ditty as he approached.

"'I am the bold Thunder,'" he quoted, as he reached his friend.

"I am, if you only knew it," said Harry to himself. "You've kept me waiting, Jack," he remarked.

"Couldn't help it; I went back for my gloves, and fell afoul of a rosy-cheeked chambermaid, who—— Hello! stop a moment, we'll have the whole county after us!"

"What now?"

"That saucy woman put me in such a temper, that, by Heaven, I walked off and forgot to pay our bill!"

"Never mind, it's paid."

"Who by? Neither you nor Midge had money enough."

"It's paid, I tell you."

"You're a jewel, Dick. Come, then, let's push on. It's ten miles to Winchester; we shall be there by eleven. You're booked for high tragedy, my boy, in this Winchester company."

"And you for comedy. I hope you'll do your part well, Rover; I have decided to play in another character."

"What the deuce do you mean? The bills are already up, with our names and parts, to play to-night at Winchester."

The good fellow was sadly taken aback when Harry told him that, for certain serious reasons of his own, he had decided to break the Winchester engagement, and that they must part there and then; nor would he listen to Rover's proposal to break his engagement also, and still keep him company.

"Have I done anything to deserve this from Dick Buskin?" asked Rover, with tears in his eyes.

"Nothing, Jack. I am your friend for life. I hate this parting as much as yourself,—but it must be. Good-by."

"I can't even bid him—— I won't, either!" cried Rover, deeply hurt. "If any cause could——"

"No cause in which you are concerned, my poor fellow; yet deep cause, for all that," said Harry, with wet eyes. "It hurts me to leave you, Jack. But—adieu!"

"Farewell, Dick; if farewell it must be."

It was with a heavy heart that Jack Rover took one road, while his late companion took another. Yet his heart was one of such native lightness that nothing could long keep it down. Chance directed his footsteps towards a locality in which were to occur events that would change the course of his whole future life. This was the vicinity of a farm-house, close by which stood an humble cottage.

The farmer was a hard-hearted and miserly fellow, named Gammon, whose chief burdens in life were that his son Sim had an honest and charitable heart, and that his daughter Jane was fond of finery and full of foolish notions. He had, indeed, a third burden, which just then was weighing upon him heavily. In the neighboring cottage dwelt a poor parson named Banks, with his sister Amelia. The farmer, whose wife had been long dead, had decided in his own mind that this lady would acceptably fill the place of the late Mrs. Gammon; but, much to his chagrin and anger, his suit had been declined. Full of revengeful inclinations, he had bought up a debt against Banks, sworn out a warrant of arrest, and placed it in the hands of a bailiff to execute.

Such was the state of affairs at the time the wandering actor, Jack Rover, approached that locality. Gammon had just ended a stormy interview with Banks, and stood fuming with rage, when his son Sim burst in, his eyes dilated with eagerness.

"O feyther!" he cried, "here's one Mr. Lamp, a ringleader of showfolks, come from Andover to act in our village. He wants a barn to play in, if you'll hire him yours."

"Surely, boy, I never refuse money. Hurry and see him before he hires some other place. Take a short cut through that garden."

"No, sir," said Mr. Banks. "You are welcome to walk in it, with my permission, but not to make it a common thoroughfare."

"Here, Sim, kick open that garden gate."

"Dang it, feyther, I can't do that!" answered Sim, rubbing his head. "I'll do anything for you that's right, feyther, but——"

"Stand aside, you idiot! I'll do it myself."

"Hold, neighbor," said Mr. Banks. "Small as this spot is, it is mine. The man who sets a foot in it against my will, must first take my life."

As they stood debating, a sudden shower of rain fell, in the midst of which Rover came running hastily towards them.

"Zounds! here's a pelting shower, and no shelter," he exclaimed. "'Poor Tom's a-cold;' I'm wet through. Oh! here's promise." He hastened towards Gammon's farm-house.

"Hold, my lad," exclaimed the farmer. "No room there for strangers. You'll find a public-house not above a mile on."

"Step in here, young man," said Mr. Banks. "My fire is small, but it burns with a welcome."

"The poor cottager! And the substantial farmer!" said Rover, looking from one to the other. He then kneeled dramatically, and quoted, "'Hear, Nature, dear goddess, hear! If ever you designed to make his corn-fields fruitful, change thy purpose; and when to town he drives his hogs, so like himself, oh, let him feel the soaking rain; then may he curse his crime too late, and know how sharper than a serpent's tooth 'tis——' Devil take me, but I'm spouting in the rain all this time!" The lively fellow sprang up and ran into the cottage, leaving Gammon, who was now in a towering rage, to solace himself with deep threats of revenge on his poor but proud neighbor.

During Rover's stay in the cottage several events of importance to our story happened. Lady Amaranth had engaged Jane, Farmer Gammon's daughter, as a waiting maid, and during the scene just described was conversing with her in the farm-house. At the same time Twitch, the bailiff employed by Gammon, appeared, and calling Mr. Banks from his cottage, served on him a warrant of arrest, on a note for thirty pounds, which the revengeful farmer had purchased.

"It is true," said Mr. Banks, "that I did borrow that sum of money, and lent it to our poor cottagers to help them pay their rents. I'll go round and see what I can collect from them."

"No, sir," answered the bailiff; "you must come with me."

"Old gentleman, come quick, or I'll draw another bottle of your currant wine," cried Rover, at this moment, from within the cottage. "Rain over, eh!" he continued, appearing at the door. "I'll take a sniff of the open air, too—— Eh, what's the matter?"

"Nothing, except that this gentleman will go to jail, unless his debt is paid," answered Twitch.

"What, my kind, hospitable, good old man to jail!" exclaimed Rover. "What's the amount, you scoundrel?"

"Better words, or I'll——"

"You'll get every bone in your body broken, rogue, if you don't tell me! Do you know, villain, that I am at this moment the greatest man living?"

"Who, pray?"

"'I am the bold Thunder!' Sirrah, know that I carry my purse of gold in my coat-pocket. Though hang me if I know how it came there!" he said, aside. "Here's twenty pictures in gold of his majesty. Take them and be off."

"Ten pieces short, master."

"Ten more! What's to be done? Ah! here's old hospitality," as Farmer Gammon entered. "Look ye, old chap, some griping rascal has had this worthy gentleman arrested. Twenty pieces of the debt is paid; you pass your word for the other ten; then, over a bottle of his currant wine, we'll drink 'liberty to the honest debtor, and confusion to the hard-hearted creditor.'"

"I shan't!" answered Gammon, curtly.

"Shan't! What's your name?"

"Gammon."

"Gammon! You're the Hampshire hog, then. I wish I had another purse in my waistcoat pocket."

The farmer withdrew in some haste, in fear lest this impetuous fellow might learn that he was the "griping rascal" referred to. At the same moment Lady Amaranth appeared from the farmhouse, and asked what was the matter.

Rover tried to tell, but found it no easy task. It was not only that the fact of his own generosity confused him, but also that the face of the beautiful Quakeress made such an impression on his mind that he had no thought for anything else. He so muddled the story that, in the end, Banks and Twitch had to come to his assistance.

"Madam, he's the honestest fellow!" cried Rover. "I've known him above forty years. He has the best hand at stirring a fire. If you were only to taste his currant wine——"

"I beg pardon, madam," broke in Mr. Banks. "I have never before needed help; but obligations from a stranger——"

"A stranger! Then, sir, thou hast assumed a right that here belongs only to me." She took a note from her purse, and attempted to repay Rover, but this he positively refused to take,

and ran hastily away, with one of his favorite
bits of dramatic quotation.

"Where dwelleth he?" asked the lady.

"I fancy where he can, madam. He seems,
from his discourse, to be a strolling actor."

"A profane stage-player, with such a gentle,
generous heart!" exclaimed Lady Amaranth. "I
should not have deemed it possible."

The good lady thereupon paid the remainder
of the debt, dismissed the bailiff, and returned
home with new thoughts in her modestly-attired
head.

The handsome face and impulsive generosity of
Rover had made an impression upon her maidenly
heart, but no deeper a one than hers had made
upon him. The whimsical fellow could not get
rid of thoughts of this sweet-faced Quakeress. He
sought the inn in an uncertain frame of mind,
now determining to go on to Winchester, now to
try his luck in a London theatre, and again to
stay where he was, and feast his eyes once more
on the face of the fair lady of bounty.

While in this state of uncertainty, the landlord
entered with the coaching-book in hand.

"Sir, you go on in the stage; what name?"

"'I am the bold Thunder,'" answered Rover,
using his favorite theatrical quotation.

"Mr. Thunder," the landlord said, writing the
name down as he walked out.

He was met outside by John Dory, who stopped
him and told him to book him for two places in

the coach. "Whom have you now?" he asked, looking over the list. "Maccolah, Gosling, Thunder.—Hillo! is there one of that name going?"

"Booked him this minute."

"What sort of a craft?"

"A rum one. I suspect he's one of the players."

"They said it was players coaxed him from school," answered John, musingly. "If this is the young squire, our journey ends before we begin it. Show me where he's moored, old purser."

Rover was just then moored in the room of Mr. Lamp, the manager of the theatrical company which had hired Farmer Gammon's barn for a week's performance. The shrewd manager well knew Rover's ability, and wanted him badly, but the stroller had fixed his mind on a London engagement, and was difficult to persuade.

"As long as I have a certain friend here, in my coat-pocket," he began, thrusting his hand in search of the purse. "Eh! where is it? Oh, the deuce! it's gone to the devil, or the bailiff, —all the same. Sir, I'll engage with you. Call a rehearsal when and where you please."

Fate, however, was preparing a change in the programme on which Rover and his new manager had not counted. As Lamp went out, John Dory came in. The worthy fellow had not seen Harry Thunder since childhood; but he had seen the name in the stage-book, and there was something in Rover's face that seemed to confirm it, so he did not hesitate to greet him with,—

"What cheer, ho, master squire?"

"Cheer, ho! my hearty," answered Rover, imitating his gruff voice.

"The very face of his father! Come, ain't you ashamed of yourself?"

"What for?" asked Rover, somewhat taken aback.

"You runaway rogue! I've dispatched a shallop to tell Lady Amaranth you're here. I expect her carriage every minute. You'll go on board, I'll go on board, and we'll drop anchor genteelly at her house; then I'll have obeyed orders, and your father will be satisfied."

"My father! Who the deuce is he? Come, good fellow, you're taking me for somebody else. Good-by."

"Avast, there! That tack won't work. They've got your name down in the stage-coach book, Mr. Thunder."

"Mr. Thunder! Ha! ha! ha! there's some odd blunder afloat."

"Take care, my lad; Sir George, your father, will change your tune."

"Sir George! Oho! my father is a knight, then! That sounds well, though he might have been an earl, and be done with it."

Rover, thinking that the joke had gone far enough, now tried to convince John Dory that he had made a mistake; but the honest fellow was

beyond conviction, and insisted vigorously on his
entering the carriage, when, shortly afterwards, it
drove up to the inn-door. By this time Rover,
in his reckless humor, was half inclined to yield
to destiny.

"Does a pretty girl sound well to your ears?"
asked John, slyly.

"Ah! this Lady Somebody is pretty, then?"

"Beautiful as a mermaid, and stately as a ship
under sail."

"And, hark ye, is this father of mine at the
lady's?"

"Afraid to face him, you runaway, are you?
No; he's in chase of a crew of deserters."

"Has the lady ever seen me?"

"None of your jokes, youngster. You know she
hasn't since you were the bigness of a canakin."

"The choice is made," said Rover, to himself.
"I have my Ranger's dress in my trunk. 'Cousin
of Buckingham, thou sage, grave man!'" he
broke out, in his theatrical humor. "To the
chariot, shipmate. 'Bear me, Bucephalus, among
the billows,—hey, for the Tigris!'"

Rover and Lady Amaranth were destined to an
agreeable surprise. On reaching his destination,
Rover was shown to a room, where he took from
his baggage his Ranger costume, the theatrical
attire of a fashionable young man. Meanwhile,
John Dory had acquainted the lady with his success. As they were still talking, Rover entered,
very handsomely dressed.

"'Tis I, Hamlet, the Dane,'" he quoted. "'Thus far into the bowels of the land have we marched on——' What! the Lady Amaranth! By Heaven, my angelic Quakeress!"

"Thou!" exclaimed the lady, turning with a warm blush on her eloquent face. "Generous youth, thou my Cousin Harry? Why, when in the village I saw thee free the lamb from the wolf, didst thou not tell me thou wert the son of my uncle, Sir George?"

"Because, my lady, then I——didn't know it myself," he concluded, mentally.

"Why didst thou vex thy father, and quit thy school?"

"'A truant disposition, good my lady, brought me from Wittenberg.'"

"Thou art tall, my cousin, and grown of comely stature. Our families have long been separated."

"Since Adam, I believe," said Rover to himself, continuing with a fragrant of stage lore: "'Then, lady, let that sweet bud of love now ripen to a beauteous flower.'"

"Love!" she exclaimed, astonished, though not altogether displeased, by the ardor of his quotation.

"'Excellent wench! perdition catch my soul, but I do love thee; and when I love thee not, chaos is come again.'"

The wild fellow rattled on in this reckless fashion, his talk more than half quotations from plays, while the pretty young Quakeress thought that, in spite of his strange humor, she had never met so pleasant a gentleman in her life as her new-found cousin. His rattle about love fell in mellow accents upon her ear, the more so that there was a depth beyond mere acting in Rover's tones. The handsome pair, indeed, bade fair, unless they were soon interrupted, to drift from sham cousin-ship into real love.

The interruption came in the form of Farmer Gammon and Lamp, the manager, their purpose being to ask the lady's permission to act a few plays in the town. The worthy pair found them-selves considerably astonished. Gammon, on being told to request permission from young Squire Thunder to lease his barn for the play, looked in Rover's face, and sneaked off. He could hope for no favor from the man whom he had recently accosted as a vagrant.

Lamp found himself in almost as great a quan-dary. Was this the Rover with whose name he had billed the country?

"Would you have a gentleman born take the part of a poor strolling dog, and help you to murder Shakespeare?" asked Rover, with an air of great severity.

"But, gentle sir, you gave your word, and I have billed your name, and trumpeted your fame for ten miles around."

"If thou hast promised, cousin," said Lady Amaranth, "thou shouldst keep thy word. I favor not play-acting, but——"

"Never in Gammon's barn, if I die for it! If play I must, it shall never be in that inhuman rogue's precincts."

"Barn! no," answered the lady. "The gallery of my house shall be thy theatre. I have invited the gentry round to my house-warming, and thou and these actors shall play before us, in spite of the grave doctrines of Ephraim Smooth."

"Thanks, my kind lady! You hear, bully Lamp? Bring your carpenters, your scene-shifters, all your lively crew; we'll show these Hampshire folks what we can do."

The sham Harry Thunder, thus masquerading in his assumed name, little dreamed of the state of affairs which had meanwhile arisen at the inn. The real Harry Thunder had reached there, having first taken a considerable round to rid himself effectually of his roving friend. As he talked with Midge in one room, Sir George entered another, out of wind and temper from his fruitless search for the deserters, and full of anger at the runaway frolic of his truant son.

As he stood fuming, and cursing the landlord, the fates, and the world in general, John Dory entered.

"John, you sea-dog!" he roared, "how now? have you taken the places in the London coach? You grin, you rascal! Have you heard anything of my son?"

"What's o'clock?" asked John, with a cunning leer.

"What the blazes does it matter?"

"Only, if it's two, Master Harry is at this minute walking with Lady Amaranth in her garden; if half after, they've east anchor to rest among the posies; if three, they're up again; if four——"

"Ahoy, you rogue! what's in your noddle, now?"

"The boy is at Lady Amaranth's, I tell you. Such a merry, crazy, crack-brained fellow,—the very picture of your honor! Bless you, if he wasn't on his knees to her in half an hour; and in an hour had his arms around her, and was giving her a bouncing smack."

"Huzza! victory!" cried Sir George, gayly. "John, you shall have a bowl for a jolly-boat, and a lake of punch to navigate in. Away with you, and order a bumper now."

Out went John, happy as an admiral, and, a minute after, in came Harry, to find his father dancing with gayety.

"I must have left my cane in this room," said Harry, looking round him. "Zounds! my father here!"

"Harry, you jackanapes! How could you shear off from the fair Quaker, and the afternoon not half spent?"

We will not repeat the conversation that ensued between father and son. It will suffice to say that it was full of cross purposes, and that by the time John Dory returned they had got themselves into a deep snarl of misunderstandings. John's presence added to the difficulty. Ignorant that this was the true Harry, he roundly declared that he had taken Sir George's son to Lady Amaranth's. Harry declared that this was false; and in the end John stamped from the room in a rage, while Sir George remained behind with his hot temper almost at boiling-point.

"You are deceiving me, you disobedient, ungrateful dog!" he roared out. "I'll not part with you till I bring you face to face with Lady Amaranth, and if I find then you've been playing on me, I'll launch you into the wide ocean of life like a dismasted pirate, without rudder, compass, grog, or tobacco."

Complicated as the situation had by this time become, it was destined to grow still more so. At Lady Amaranth's house Rover had made such happy use of his time that nearly all the household was pressed into the service of the actors, and servants and maids were diligently conning their parts. Even Lady Amaranth had consented to study the part of Rosalind, in "As You Like It," while Ephraim Smooth was nearly alone in his horrified distaste to the play.

"Why dost thou suffer him," he said to Lady Amaranth, "to put into the hands of thy servants books of tragedies and books of comedies, prelude, interlude, yea, all lewd? My spirit doth wax wroth. Verily, a play-book is the primer of Beelzebub."

"Listen, while I read from one," answered

Lady Amaranth. "'Not the king's crown, nor the deputed sword, the marshal's truncheon, nor the judge's robe, become them with one-half so good a grace as mercy does.' Doth Beelzebub speak such words as these?"

Before Ephraim could reply, the sound of a violin was heard without. The horrified zealot closed both ears with his hands, while a look of dismal distress overspread his long-drawn face.

"I must shut my ears," he groaned. "The man of sin rubbeth the hair of the horse to the bowels of the cat."

"Now, if agreeable to your ladyship, we'll go over your song," said Lamp, who at that moment entered, violin in hand. Rover came close behind him.

"I will go over it!" cried Ephraim, in a rage, as he snatched the book from Lady Amaranth's hand, flung it to the floor, and trampled upon it.

"Trample on Shakespeare!" exclaimed Rover, thrusting him violently back. "'You sacrilegious thief, that from a shelf the precious diadem stole, and put it in your pocket!'" He picked up the book. "Go on, my lady. Silence, 'thou owl of Crete.'"

Ephraim, however, was not to be silenced, and became so violent in his language that Rover ended by hustling him from the room. The rehearsal then proceeded peacefully. At its conclusion, Lamp and his fair pupil withdrew, leaving Rover alone.

"An angel in drab!" he said to himself. "In all my roving I never saw her like. If Sir George don't soon arrive, to denounce me as an impostor, I'll be tempted to marry my lovely Rosalind. Shall I, though? No, no, I can't play the scoundrel,—not with her. Poor Dick Buskin wants money more than I, yet he'd hang himself rather than do such a scurvy deed, and I'll do nothing to make him ashamed of me."

Even as he spoke, the person he had just named entered the room, and started with surprise on recognizing his friend Rover.

"Heigho! I don't know what to do," sighed Rover.

"Nor what to say," said Harry, in the same dismal tone.

"Dick Buskin, by the gods!" cried Rover, turning suddenly. "My dear fellow! Ha! ha! ha! talk of the devil, and—— I was just thinking of you. 'Pon my soul, Dick, I'm so happy to see you!"

"But, Jack, how came you to find me out?"

"Find you? It's you that has found me out. Has the news of my intended play brought you?"

"He doesn't know me, then," said Harry to himself. "Egad! I'll carry on the joke."

If Rover did not know Harry's secret, Harry soon knew Rover's, for the latter quickly told him the story of his masquerade, and his belief that, as Harry Thunder, he had won the heart of a charming lady. He went on to say that she thought him a gentleman, and that, as he was a man of honor, she should never despise him as a rascal; declaring that he would finish with the play, and then bid her forever adieu in his true character of Jack Rover.

"The same generous, honest fellow as ever. He shan't lose by it, if I can help him to win the woman," said Harry to himself; and, moved by a sudden impulse, he told Rover a story that did more honor to his invention than his truthfulness.

This story was that Rover had anticipated him, since he had come there for the same purpose, of passing himself on the lady as Harry Thunder. He had gone even beyond this, he said, and brought with him a sham father to personate the simon-pure Sir George,—an "old-man" comedian, who could play the irascible father to perfection.

"The impudent old scoundrel!" cried Rover. "I'll step down-stairs and have the honor of—— I'll kick him."

"No, no, Rover. I brought him into it, and won't have him hurt."

"What's his name?"

"His name is—is—Abrawang."

"Abrawang! Never heard of the man. Ha! ha! two Squire Thunders in the field, and both rogues!"

"Hark ye, Jack. I'm ashamed of myself, and want you to punish me and my confederate. Suppose you keep up the character of young Squire Thunder. You can easily do it, and——"

"But, by Heaven, I'll——— 'Quoit him down, Bardolph.'"

"You love her, Jack; she loves you; her fortune is a snug one. If you can marry her———"

"She's lovely, Dick; but hang her fortune! 'My love, more noble than the world, prizes not quantity of dirty lands.'"

Harry was in solid earnest, and took immediate steps to carry out the plot he had so hastily formed, with the ardent and generous desire to advance the fortunes of his friend, if even at his own possible loss.

He met Lady Amaranth a few minutes after parting with Rover, and told her a somewhat different story from that which he had invented for the latter. To her, Sir George must continue Sir George, but as for himself, he was simply Dick Buskin, a strolling player, and a confederate of the old knight in a scheme of rascality. Sir George, said the graceless youth, had grown so angry with his son for his irregular conduct that to punish him he had determined to treat him as an impostor, in the hope that she might drive him from her presence. He, Dick Buskin, had agreed to represent the real son, but his conscience had so smitten him that he felt obliged to acquaint the lady with the imposture. He had already told Harry of it, and advised him to punish Sir George by treating him himself as an impostor.

"Ha! ha! ha!" laughed Lady Amaranth, in mirthful enjoyment of this fiction. "That will be a just retaliation on my uncle for his cruel intentions, both to his son and me."

They were interrupted at this juncture by Sir George, who entered as they were talking, and bade his reluctant son to salute his lady cousin.

"Here, my lady," he said, as they both held back, "take from a father's hand, Harry Thunder."

"That I may not," answered Lady Amaranth, turning to Rover, who had just then entered. Taking his hand, she said, "Here, sir, take from *my* hand, Harry Thunder."

"Eh!" exclaimed Sir George, staring at Rover, who stared at him in return.

"Oh! this is your sham Sir George?" said Rover, aside to Harry.

"Yes; I've told the lady, and she'll seem to humor him."

"I shan't, though," rejoined Rover. He turned to Sir George, and said in a tone of satire, "How do you do, Abrawang?"

"Abrawang!" exclaimed Sir George, with a start of surprise.

"Ay, that's very well done. Never lose sight of your character. Sir George, you know, is a noisy, turbulent, wicked old seaman. Angry? bravo!—pout your under lip, purse your brows,—very well done!" By this time Sir George was stamping about the room in a passion. "Very good! that's right! strut about on your little pegs!" and Rover clapped his hands approvingly.

"I'm in such a fury!" cried the old man.

"We know that. I never saw a happier low comedy figure. Why, only show yourself like that, and you'll set an audience in a roar."

"'Sblood and fire!'"

"Who is this?" asked Lady Amaranth, pointing to Rover.

"Some puppy unknown."

"And thou dost not know this gentleman?" she pointed to Sir George.

"'Excellent well; he's a fish-monger.'"

"And this youth?" pointing to Harry.

"'My friend Horatio! I wear thee in my heart's core; yea, in my heart of hearts',—as I do thee," and the impulsive fellow embraced Lady Amaranth.

This freedom with his niece increased Sir George's rage almost to a frenzy. Rover continued to twit him, till in the end the furious old gentleman raised his cane and used it freely, some of the actors who had entered, his son, and Rover, coming in for a share of his favors. In the end, he stamped in a hot rage from the room.

Here was an indignity to which the light-hearted stroller had not been accustomed. His honor was to him his most valued possession, and in a moment his mood changed from merriment to an ardent desire for revenge.

"A rascally old impostor stigmatize me with a blow!" he cried. "Zounds! I'll follow him! 'and may the name of villain light on me' if I don't bang—Mr. Abrawang!"

Leaving time to clear up this complicated intrigue, we must now follow the current of events to the locality of the farm-house and the cottage, where the miserly farmer had devised a new scheme of revenge against his poor neighbor. Though the debt of Mr. Banks had been paid, he was still behindhand in his rent, and Gammon took advantage of this fact to turn him out-of-doors and seize his furniture, which he placed in charge of a sheriff's officer.

The distressed cottager, not knowing what to do, took his sister to Lady Amaranth, requesting that generous lady to give her shelter until he could find her another home. This request was promptly granted, and Lady Amaranth, in addition, promised to protect them against the greed of their miserly landlord.

Sim, the farmer's son, had been ordered, much against his will, to make an inventory of Mr. Banks's goods and chattels. This he dutifully performed, but, in his goodness of heart, secretly offered the poor man his own and his sister's savings to pay his debt,—a generous offer which the grateful cottager could not accept. About the same time, in the immediate neighborhood of the cottage, Sir George Thunder was experiencing a series of exciting adventures. Wandering thitherward to cool his rage, he had come in sight of three villanous-looking fellows, dressed as sailors, whom he believed to be the deserters of whom he was in search. On perceiving him, they took refuge in a piece of woodland. Without thought of consequences, he was about to follow them, when he was stopped by Rover, who had traced him to this point. The angry actor charged him with having wounded his honor, and hotly demanded redress.

"The English of all this is that we're to fight," answered Sir George. "Well, I've only one objection to fighting you."

"What's that, sir?"

"That you seem too brave a lad to be killed."

"Sir, at present I wear the stigma of a coward."

"Zounds! I like a bit of fighting. I don't know when I've smelt gunpowder,—except to bring down a woodcock. I would not wish to destroy what was built for good service; but, hang me, if I don't wing you, to teach you better manners!"

Rover was thoroughly in earnest. He produced a pair of pistols, gave one to Sir George, and walked to a convenient distance with the other. In a moment more those mistaken hot-heads would have been firing at one another, but for an unexpected interruption. As Sir George stood loading his weapon, the ruffians who had taken refuge in the wood, and who had not seen Rover, rushed out and assailed the old baronet, one of them snatching the pistol from his hand.

"You are the old pirate that has chased us all over the country," cried the man, spitefully. "You wanted our lives, did you? We'll have yours, you bandy-legged old rascal!"

He aimed the pistol at Sir George, but before he could fire Rover ran up, dashed the weapon from his hand, and covered the villains with his own weapon.

"Hold up there, rascals!" he cried.

The villains, on seeing the tables thus turned, made a hasty dash for the wood, followed closely by Rover. Sir George seized the other pistol and was about to follow, when John Dory appeared and threw his arms around him.

"You shan't go a step," cried the old salt.

"Let me go! Hear that?" A pistol-shot came from the wood. "The brave lad saved my life. Let me go."

"I'll save your life!" exclaimed John, whipping his diminutive master up in his arms. "I'm your guardian, you old sea-dog, and can't let you throw yourself away on such piratical craft as these."

The old tar's untimely interference left Rover in serious danger. After he had ineffectively discharged his weapon, the deserters set upon him, and handled him so roughly that only the superior agility of his legs saved his head from being beaten into a jelly. Escaping from them with difficulty, his flying footsteps brought him to Mr. Banks's cottage, which he entered faint with exhaustion. He leaned against the wall for support, while Amelia, the cottager's sister, who had returned thither, came to his aid, asking earnestly if he was hurt.

Rover told her, in a few words, what had happened, and begged her for a glass of her currant wine, of whose enlivening properties he knew from former experience. The good lady looked at him with emotion. Something in his face touched her heart, and the sound of his voice seemed to rouse long-buried recollections in her soul.

Rover was yet, however, far from through with his adventures. As ne sat talking with the lady, the sheriff's officer who had been placed in charge of the house entered the room, where he behaved so rudely that the high-tempered young actor snatched up a cane and drove him from the house. Rover followed in a high passion,—but only to find himself in a new difficulty. The three ruffians had pursued him to the cottage, with cries of "stop thief!" On their way thither they were joined by a number of countrymen, to whom they declared that they had been robbed. As Rover dashed from the cottage in pursuit of the insulting officer, he found himself in the midst of this throng, and was at once seized, bound, and dragged away to Lady Amaranth's, the villains swearing roundly that he was a highwayman, and must be placed in the hands of justice at once.

Sir George had reached the house of the lady of the manor in much the same manner, being borne thither in the arms of John Dory, as Ephraim Smooth said, " like a shrimp in the claws of a blue lobster."

Mr. Banks and his sister Amelia, learning of Rover's capture, quickly sought the same locality, and entered the room occupied by Sir George and John Dory while the ruffled knight was still roaring out his opinion of the old sailor.

"Rascal! to whip me up like a pound of tea, dance me about like a young bear, and make me desert the preserver of my life! What will puppy unknown think of me?"

"No matter what; out to-night you shall not budge," said John, resolutely.

As he spoke he wheeled half round, and his eyes fell on Amelia. They half started from his head on perceiving her, while his legs shook like saplings in a gale.

"Oh! marcy of Heaven!" exclaimed the thunderstruck old tar. "Isn't it? Oh, master! Look! look!"

Amelia faced them at this exclamation, and seeing Sir George, gave vent to a cry of deep emotion, and fell half fainting into the arms of Lady Amaranth, who had just entered.

"Great Heaven! It is Amelia!" cried Sir George, as full of consternation as his old boatswain had been.

He seized her hand, and with strong emotion begged her forgiveness for the wrong he had done her, vowing that he had been a deep villain, and would marry her now as the only reparation in his power. Mr. Banks now stepped forward with dignity and told him that in this respect he was deceived, that the marriage ceremony had been performed by himself, and was a legal one, and that the lady was his true wife.

Sir George stood dazed at this confirmation of what John Dory had already told him, but which he had not believed, and in a faint voice asked Amelia concerning her son, his infant heir.

" Ah, husband, he—alas !"

" Gone ? What a miserable scoundrel I've been ! My true heir dead, and Harry an undutiful cub. By Jove, I'll adopt that brave lad, who wouldn't let anybody kill me but himself. Marry him, my Lady Amaranth. He is a fine fellow, and shall have my estate."

They were interrupted in this happy reconciliation by news that a footpad had been captured, and that the men he had robbed stood ready to give evidence against him.

" Leave them to me," cried Sir George, bustling into the room where they were. " Oh, ho ! Clap down the hatches ! Secure these sharks !" he roared, as he cast his eyes on the ruffians. " So the rogues have run their heads into the lion's mouth ! Release that young man. Keep these fellows in limbo. They are deserters from the King's navy."

The villains, thus opportunely discovered, were carried off prisoners, while John Dory cut the ropes from Rover's hands, roaring out, " My young master ! What in Davy Jones's name have you been at now ?"

"My cousin Harry!" exclaimed Lady Amaranth.

"Not quite, madam," answered Rover, as the true Harry entered, and gazed with surprise on the scene. "As I told this worthy tar, when he first forced me to your house, I am not the son of Sir George Thunder."

"You refuse the lady!" said Harry. "Then, to punish you, I've half a mind to take her myself."

"Stop, Dick, that won't work. Madam, don't listen to this fellow. He is as much of an impostor as myself. Isn't he, Abrawang?"

"Not so, my dear Rover," answered Harry, with a laugh. "I have been fooling you and teasing my father long enough. When I joined your company I was a runaway school-boy, and my true name is Harry Thunder."

"Must I believe all this?" said Rover. "Who, then, is Abrawang? Madam, is your uncle, Sir George Thunder, in this room?"

"He is," said Lady Amaranth, pointing to Sir George.

"Then what a ridiculous part you've made me play between you!" cried Rover, angrily. "This old shark swore I was Harry Thunder; and forced me to deceive this noble lady. I sincerely beg her forgiveness. And this young runaway vowed he was a fraud, and his father a low comedian. Sir George, I beg your pardon; and hope you'll apologize to me."

"That I will, my noble splinter. Now tell me

from what dock you were launched, my heart of oak."

Rover answered that he was but a waif, born, he believed, in England, but left astray, from his earliest recollection, in the East Indies. The lady in whose charge he was as a child had perished during the troubles in that region, leaving him in the care of a sergeant's wife. As he grew up he had learned to act in the Calcutta theatre, and from there had come to England, assuming the name of Rover, and hoping to find his parents in his native land.

"Can you remember the name of the town where——" began Amelia, in deep agitation.

"It was the town of Negapatam, madam."

"And of the lady in whose care you were left?"

"She was the wife of a Major Linstock. But I have heard that my mother's name was Scymour."

"Merciful Heaven! it is my son!" cried the deeply-moved lady. "My Charles! my long-lost son!" She embraced him warmly. "You have found your parents, my boy, for there stands your father," pointing to Sir George.

"He! can it be? He, against whose life I raised my hand!"

"My brave boy; it does my heart good to find I have a son with the spirit to fight me as a stranger, yet defend me as a father," cried Sir George.

"And that I have found a brother in the man who won my heart as a comrade stroller," said Harry, warmly pressing Rover's hand.

"And I a lover in the warm-hearted actor," said Lady Amaranth, taking his other hand. "Sir George, you shall not disinherit Harry; I have fortune enough to make your son Charles rich."

"And love enough, I know, to make him the happiest benedict in England," cried Rover, gayly. "Now for the play. Call Lamp, our lusty manager. My 'Wild Oats' are all sown, and the rest of my life shall be," he continued, turning to Lady Amaranth, "'As You Like it.'"

THE SCHOOL FOR SCANDAL.

BY RICHARD BRINSLEY BUTLER SHERIDAN.

[WE do not feel called upon to say much about
the author of this celebrated comedy. The story
of the life of Richard Brinsley Sheridan is too
well known to demand extended comment. It
will suffice to say that he was born at Dublin in
1751, acquired at school the reputation of being
an "impenetrable dunce," married Miss Linley,
a noted songstress, in 1772,—a marriage made
notable by an elopement and a duel,—and first
appeared as a playwright in 1775, with the amusing comedy of "The Rivals." His greatest play,
"The School for Scandal," appeared in 1777. He
also · wrote a musical drama, "The Duenna,"
which was highly successful, a farce called "The
Critic," and some smaller dramatic works, besides
translating Kotzebue's plays, "The Stranger" and
"Pizarro." Sheridan attained no less fame as an
orator than as a dramatist. During much of his
life he was a member of Parliament, or otherwise
connected with the government, while his celebrated speech on the impeachment trial of Warren Hastings is still regarded as one of the most

156

splendid examples of oratory ever given. His private life was one of such extravagance that he was rarely free from debt, and in his later years he became greatly embarrassed. He died in 1816.

Of English wits Sheridan stands almost at the head, and to its overflowing fund of witty dialogue the "School for Scandal" owes much of its enduring popularity; though this is largely due, also, to the interest of the plot and the high dramatic merit of many of the situations. In its incessant coruscation of sparkling repartee this play is only rivalled by the dramas of Congreve, whose merit resides chiefly in the brilliancy of their dialogue. As we have given no example of Congreve's genius, for reasons already explained, we repair the omission by presenting the stories of two of Sheridan's plays, "The School for Scandal" and "The Rivals," both of which retain their popularity to a remarkable extent, and continue among the most frequently acted examples of the older English drama.]

Charles and Joseph Surface, the nephews of Sir Oliver Surface, a rich merchant of India, displayed that difference in character which is so often manifested between brothers. Joseph was discreet, cautious, and economical, and his conversation full of moral sentiments and professions of benevolence. Yet his morality and charity were only in words, and his secret feelings were those of the heartless and selfish libertine. Charles, on the contrary, sadly lacked discretion and economy. His days and nights were passed in the pursuits of the spendthrift, in which the estate his father had left him, and the money his uncle had sent him, had been recklessly squandered. Of his once abundant means he had nothing left but his house and furniture, while he was deeply in debt. Yet his feelings were as warm as those of his brother were cold, he was lavishly generous, and was ready at any appeal to give in charity the money that should have been used to pay his debts.

These young men had their separate love affairs, which may be briefly described. Charles was warmly in love with a beautiful young lady named Maria, who in her heart returned his affection, but repelled his suit through her dislike to his dissolute habits. Joseph professed to love the same young lady, but his affection was really placed upon her money, for she was the heiress to a considerable estate, her guardian being an old knight named Sir Peter Teazle, who had also acted as guardian to the two brothers.

Charles had also won the affection of a Lady Sneerwell, though of this he was quite unaware. This lady was a prominent member of a group of busy scandal-mongers, which included also Mrs. Candour, Sir Benjamin Backbite, Mr. Crabtree, his father, Mr. Snake, and others. The principal aim in life of these personages seemed to be the retailing of scandalous stories, of which their nearest friends were often the victims, none being so pure in life but that they could pick holes in their characters, no story so innocent but that they could throw on it some shadow of double meaning. As for Lady Sneerwell, her leading design was to break off the love affair between Charles and Maria, by whispering into the young lady's ear rumors of her lover's libertine career. Her secret hope was that, through success in this insidious effort, she might catch his heart in the rebound.

Sir Peter Teazle, of whom we have above spoken, has so much to do with our story that we must say more concerning him. He was a wealthy gentleman of advanced years, who had recently married a beautiful young wife, a girl of country birth and education, but whose head had been turned by the glamour of London life. Brought up in comparative poverty, her extravagance as a fashionable lady kept her in constant hot water with her husband, their life being a series of quarrels and reconciliations. In addition to her extravagance, Lady Teazle became an active member of the school for scandal, in which Lady Sneerwell and Mrs. Candour were the leading professors, and soon grew to be as apt as any of them in their peculiar art. In her heedless gayety she even exposed herself to the slanderous tongues of her associates, for Joseph Surface had made an insidious assault upon her virtue, and she was too thoughtless to perceive into what unpleasant complications her penchant for him might lead her.

At heart, however, Lady Teazle had the sturdy virtue of her country training, and was not likely to be led astray by the wiles of her libertine lover.

At the time our story opens, Sir Oliver Surface, the uncle of the two young men, had just arrived in London, though this was not known to his nephews. It was a secret known only to Rowley, an old servant of the family, and to Sir Peter Teazle, to whom Rowley revealed it. In fact, Sir Oliver had come to London for a special purpose. He had already liberally supplied his nephews with money, and was ready to help them further, for they were his only near relations, but before doing so he wished to gain a personal knowledge of their characters, and discover which of the two was most worthy to be made his heir. As for Sir Peter, he was likely to prove a biassed advocate, for he believed firmly in Joseph, whose moral sentiments seemed to him the true coin of sterling honesty; while the extravagance of the other nephew had made an enemy of the old knight. Rowley, on the other hand, had a deeper insight into the true characters of the two young men, and earnestly upheld the merit of Charles. But Sir Oliver was not the man to take anything at second-hand; he resolved to test his nephews for himself, with Rowley's aid, and decide which was best suited to be the recipient of his bounty.

Sir Oliver had reached London at a fortunate time for Charles Surface, if he was to be saved from utter ruin. He had sold everything in his house to raise money, except the family pictures, and was so deeply in debt to Jews and tradesmen that, as Sir Benjamin Backbite told the members of the scandalous college, "when he entertained his friends he would sit down to dinner with a dozen of his own securities, have a score of tradesmen waiting in the antechamber, and an officer behind every guest's chair."

Our first acquaintance with the characters whom we have introduced to the reader must be made in the house of Sir Peter Teazle, who, on our entrance, has just completed his daily quarrel with his wife. He had attempted to take her to task for her extravagance and her association with the scandal-mongers, but had failed, as usual, to bring her to a sense of wrong-doing.

"So, I have gained much by my intended expostulation," he said to himself, after she had left the room. "Yet with what a charming air she contradicts everything I say, and how pleasantly she shows her contempt for my authority! Well, though I can't make her love me, there is great satisfaction in quarrelling with her; and I think she never appears to such advantage as when she is doing everything in her power to plague me."

Lady Teazle showed her appreciation of her husband's good advice by going directly to Lady Sneerwell's house, where she found the whole tribe of slanderers assembled, and busily engaged in dissecting the characters of their friends. Maria, who was present, attempted some gentle expostulation, but her words were wasted, the tide of scandal continuing to flow until it was quite exhausted.

After these earnest laborers in a bad cause had left the room, Joseph Surface and Maria remained, an opportunity of which he at once took advantage to press his suit with the young lady. Unluckily for his plans, Lady Teazle returned while he was on his knees before her, and found him in that embarrassing position.

Here was a serious dilemma for the double-dealing Joseph! How should he remove Lady Teazle's suspicions and retain her favor? He managed to get Maria from the room, and then sought, by the first lie that came into his head, to explain his tender attitude. His effort was not so successful as he had hoped. Lady Teazle affected to close her eyes, but was by no means blinded, and after her departure her plotting lover exclaimed,—

"A curious dilemma, truly, my politics have run me into! I begin to wish I had never made such a point of gaining so very good a character, for it has led me into so many cursed rogueries that I doubt I shall be exposed at last."

Meanwhile Rowley had brought Sir Oliver to the house of Sir Peter Teazle, for an interview concerning his graceless nephews, having first warned him that he would find his old friend

greatly prejudiced against his nephew Charles.
But he assured him that this was largely due to
jealousy, and that Lady Sneerwell, for her own
purposes, had done her best to set afloat a story
of illicit relations between Charles Surface and
Lady Teazle. In this choice bit of scandal
she had been fully aided by her associates,—
though Rowley's opinion was that if the lady
cared for either of the brothers it was for Joseph.

"I am not to be prejudiced against my nephew
by such a set of malicious, prating gossips, who
murder characters to kill time," declared Sir
Oliver. "No, no; if Charles has done nothing
false or mean, I shall compound for his extravagance."

Sir Peter's opinion fully justified Rowley's
warning. He assured Sir Oliver that Charles
was a lost young man, and that Joseph was a
model of prudence and morality.

"You will be convinced of this when you meet
this discreet young man," declared Sir Peter. "It
is edification to hear him converse; he professes
the noblest sentiments."

"Oh, plague of his sentiments!" exclaimed Sir
Oliver. "If he salutes me with a scrap of morality
in his mouth I shall be sick directly. I don't
mean to defend Charles's errors, Sir Peter; but
before I form my judgment of either of them I
intend to make a trial of their hearts. My friend
Rowley and I have planned something for that
purpose."

This plan, which he proceeded to unfold to Sir Peter, was the following: A Dublin merchant, named Stanley, who was nearly related to the mother of the two young men, had been unfortunate in business and was imprisoned for debt. He had written to the brothers for assistance, but had received nothing in return, though Charles was trying to raise a sum of money for his relief. Rowley's plan was to inform the two brothers that Mr. Stanley had gained permission to apply in person to his friends. This done, Sir Oliver would call upon them in the character of Stanley, and by an appeal to their benevolence seek to gain some insight into their dispositions.

Further consideration, however, induced Sir Oliver to change this plan, so far as Charles was concerned, and call upon him under another character. A money-lending Jew, named Moses, who was well acquainted with the affairs of the young profligate, had been requested to call at Sir Peter's house, and give the uncle some exact information as to the true state of his nephew's financial situation.

The story Moses told was to the effect that Charles's fortune was just then some thousands of pounds on the wrong side of nothing. But this, he said, was not known to all the money-lenders of the city, and he had engaged to bring that very evening a gentleman named Premium, who would advance the young man some money. On hearing this, Sir Peter at once suggested that it would be an excellent plan for Sir Oliver to represent Mr. Premium, since he might thus see his nephew in all his glory.

"Egad, I like this plan better than the other?" declared Sir Oliver. "And I may visit Joseph afterwards as old Stanley."

"This is taking Charles rather at a disadvantage," protested Rowley. "But be it so; I have no fear for him."

Moses hereupon instructed Sir Oliver how he must play his part as a money-lender. The principal necessity was that he should be exorbitant enough in his demands. If his client appeared not very anxious, he might lend him money at forty or fifty per cent., but if he appeared in great distress he might ask double. Then, he must not have the moneys himself, but must have to borrow them from a friend. This friend must be an unconscionable dog, who had not the moneys by him, but was forced to sell stock at a great loss to obtain them. These and other instructions fairly prepared Sir Oliver for the part he was to play, and he left the house with Moses, quite ready to carry out this well-devised plot.

Hardly had they gone when Maria entered. Her guardian, who was well aware of her relations to the two brothers, took advantage of the opportunity to contrast to her their characters, and strongly advised her to give up all thoughts of the dissolute Charles, and yield to the addresses of the moral and amiable Joseph. His advice

was wasted. Maria was not to be moved. In
the end he lost his temper at her obstinacy, and
sternly ordered her from the room, sourly declaring to himself that her father had died only to
plague him with the care of his perverse daughter.

Sir Peter was not yet through with his morning's frets. His interview with Maria was followed by one with his wife, which ended no
more happily. Lady Teazle, indeed, made her
appearance in an excellent humor, and they
began in the most lover-like mood, resolving to
quarrel no more, and to live thereafter like turtle-
doves.

" But, my dear Lady Teazle, you must watch
your temper very seriously," warned Sir Peter,
" for in all our little quarrels, my dear, if you
recollect, my love, you always began first."

" I beg your pardon, my dear Sir Peter : indeed,
you always gave the provocation."

" Now, see, my angel, take care,—contradicting
isn't the way to keep friends."

" Then don't you begin it, my love."

" There, now, you—you are going on. You
don't perceive, my life, that you are just doing
the very thing which you know always makes me
angry."

" Nay, you know if you will be angry without
any reason, my dear——"

" There, now ! who begins first ?"

" Why, you, to be sure. I said nothing,—but
there is no bearing your temper."

"No, no, madam; the fault's in your own temper."

And on it went until the pair, who had been ardent lovers ten minutes before, were in such a furious quarrel that Sir Peter vowed that nothing would content him but a divorce.

"Agreed, agreed," cried Lady Teazle, merrily. "And now, my dear Sir Peter, we are of a mind once more, and may be the happiest couple and never differ again, you know; ha! ha! ha! Well, you are going to be in a passion, I see, and I shall only interrupt you,—so, by! by!"

"Plagues and tortures! can't I make her angry either?" he cried, as she ran laughing from the room. "I'll not bear her presuming to keep her temper! No, she may break my heart, but she shan't keep her temper!" and he stamped angrily out after her.

Meanwhile Sir Oliver was on his way, under the guidance of Moses, to the residence of Charles Surface.

That gentleman was not occupied as a ruined person might be supposed to be. On the contrary, he was in the highest of spirits, enjoying himself with a group of his boon companions, drinking and singing, and seemingly miles away from the shadow of disaster.

Yet this shadow was not far removed. When the young spendthrift was called from the room by the visit of the Jew and the assumed money-broker, and asked what security he had to offer for the money he wished to borrow, he could think of nothing but his expectations from the estate of his rich uncle.

"They tell me I am a prodigious favorite, and that he talks of leaving me everything," he declared.

"Indeed! that is the first I've heard of it," answered Sir Oliver.

"It's so, indeed. At the same time he has been so liberal to me that I should be very sorry to hear that anything had happened to him."

"No more than I should," exclaimed Sir Oliver. "I assure you of that. But I am told that he is very hale and hearty."

"Not at all," declared Charles. "He breaks apace, I am told,—and is so much altered lately that his nearest relations would not know him."

This remark threw Sir Oliver into such a fit of laughter that Charles looked at him in surprise. He could not imagine what Mr. Premium, as he supposed him to be, could see so amusing in his words. At the end, however, Sir Oliver, in his character of broker, asked him if there was no other security he could offer? What had become of the rich old plate his father had left, and the valuable library? Charles answered lightly that the plate had gone to the Jews and the books to the auctioneer long ago, and that nothing remained of the family property but a room full of ancestors. These he would sell him at a bargain, if he had a taste for old pictures.

"What! you wouldn't sell your forefathers, would you?" exclaimed Sir Oliver.

"Every man of them, to the best bidder."

"What! your great-uncles and aunts?"

"Yes, and my great-grandfathers and grandmothers, too."

A groan came from Sir Oliver at this. "The heartless profligate!" he said to himself. "I'll never forgive him this! never!"

Charles, however, insisted on the sale, enlisting Careless, one of his boon companions, to act as auctioneer, and the party adjourned to the picture gallery with the purpose of disposing of the family portraits.

"When a man wants money, where the plague should he get assistance if he can't make free with his own relations?" asked Charles, gayly. "But, Gad's life, little Premium, you don't seem to like the business."

"Oh, yes, I do, vastly. Ha! ha! ha! yes, yes, I think it a rare joke to sell one's family by auction—ha! ha!" Then in an undertone he groaned out, "Oh, the prodigal! I'll never forgive him; never!"

Entering the gallery, whose walls were adorned with a goodly show of portraits, many of them of value as paintings, Careless mounted a gouty old chair as auctioneer's stand, rolled up a genealogical tree of the family as auctioneer's hammer, and proceeded to knock off the portraits as

Charles called them out and Sir Oliver made his bids.

The sale proceeded till a goodly number of the pictures had been disposed of at fair prices. By this time, however, Charles had grown tired of the sport, and he proposed to sell all the remainder of the family in the lump, for three hundred pounds.

"Well, well, anything to accommodate you," said Sir Oliver; "they are mine. But there is one portrait which you have always passed over."

"What, that ill-looking little fellow over the settee?" asked Careless.

"Yes, sir, I mean that; though I don't think him so ill-looking a little fellow, by any means."

"What, that?" said Charles. "Oh, that's my uncle Oliver. It was done before he went to India."

"Ah! and I suppose uncle Oliver goes with the rest of the lumber."

"No, hang it! I'll not part with poor Noll. The old fellow has been very good to me, and, egad, I'll keep his picture while I've a room to put it in."

"The rogue's my nephew after all!" said Sir Oliver to himself. "I must forgive him—— But I have somehow taken a fancy to that picture," he declared aloud.

"I'm sorry for that, for you can't have it. Haven't you got enough of them?"

"But, sir, I don't value money when I take a

whim. I'll give you as much for that as for all the rest."

"Don't tease me, master broker," cried Charles. "I tell you I'll not part with it, and there's an end of it."

Importunity proved unavailing, and the counterfeit broker took his leave, after giving his check for the purchase-money. At heart he was delighted to find that his profligate nephew thought so highly of him as to refuse ten times its value for his picture.

"The dear extravagant rogue!" he said to himself. "Let me hear now who dares call him profligate!"

As for Charles, he quickly performed an act that was likely to bring him still more into his uncle's favor. For, meeting Rowley, he insisted on giving him a hundred pounds of the money he had just received, to be sent to Mr. Stanley. Rowley objected to this, advising him to be just before he was generous, but the impulsive young man would listen to no remonstrance, and fairly forced him to accept the money. This act of charity Rowley soon told to Sir Oliver, who was so greatly pleased on hearing it that he vowed he would pay the young rogue's debts and his charities as well.

It remained for the uncle to call on his other nephew, in his assumed character of Mr. Stanley. But before he could do this, the standing of Joseph as a moralist was greatly injured by certain unlucky circumstances, prepared for him, as it seemed, by the adverse fates. These circumstances we have next to describe.

Lady Teazle, in her desire to conform to all the follies of fashion, was in the habit of visiting Joseph Surface clandestinely, and on the day in question had agreed to call upon him. A knock coming upon the door of the library, in which room he awaited her, he bade the servant to draw a screen before the window as a guard against the possible curiosity of his neighbor, and then told him to admit the visitor.

It proved to be Lady Teazle, as he had suspected. She had left her chair at the milliner's in the next street, and come on foot to his house, more through foolish perversity than from any wrong intention. But Joseph's purpose was much less innocent than hers. He wished to get her into his power, that he might use her in the furtherance of his other schemes. Unluckily for him, a most awkward circumstance came to pass. In the midst of his moral arguments to prove that wrong is right, the servant hastily entered and announced that Sir Peter was on the stairs and coming to the room.

This news created an instant consternation. It was too late for Lady Teazle to escape by the door, and no place of shelter appeared but behind the screen. Here she hastily hid herself, in the hope that the unwelcome visitor would soon depart, and vowing never to be caught in such a scrape again. As for Joseph, he seized a book, and when Sir Peter entered appeared to be so absorbed in reading that the visitor had to tap him on the shoulder to bring him to himself.

This evident desire for knowledge on the part of his moral *protégé* so pleased the old gentleman that he highly commended his studious habits. He concluded by telling him that the purpose of his visit was to confide to him an important family secret.

Joseph just then would have given no small sum of money to have had Lady Teazle out of the way, for he feared the character of Sir Peter's communication. But there was no help for it. The lady was there, and her husband could not be hushed. The fox was fairly caught in his own trap, and was obliged to sit and listen to a revelation that threatened to be ruinous to his base purposes.

Sir Peter began by saying that Lady Teazle's conduct of late had made him very unhappy. He suspected her of having formed an attachment to another, and that other no less than the libertine Charles Surface. This statement Joseph heard with an assurance of the deepest regret. He could scarcely credit, he declared, that his brother could be capable of such baseness. And it was not possible for him, he concluded, to suspect Lady Teazle's honor.

Sir Peter thanked him for his noble sentiments, and proceeded to say that he wished to think

15*

well of his wife, and intended to remove one of
the chief causes of their frequent disputes. They
differed in their ideas of expense, but he had resolved to provide her with an income of her own.
It was his purpose to settle on her eight hundred
pounds a year during his life. More than this,
he had drawn up another paper which would
settle the bulk of his fortune on her at his death,
—but this fact he desired Joseph to keep a strict
secret.

Unfortunately for Joseph's purposes the secret
was already out. Lady Teazle had heard every
word of her husband's generous intentions. Sir
Peter now proceeded to talk on as awkward a
theme, for he strongly advocated a matrimonial
alliance between Joseph and his ward Maria. This
untimely outflow of confidences was at length
interrupted by the entrance of the servant, who
announced that Charles Surface was below.

" A thought has struck me," exclaimed Sir Peter.
" Before Charles enters, conceal me somewhere,
and then do you tax him on the point we were
talking of. His answer may satisfy me at once.
Here, this screen will do." Before Joseph could
stop him he had advanced to the screen and
caught a glimpse behind it. " Hey! what the
devil!" he cried. " There seems to be one listener
here already—— I'll swear I saw a petticoat!"

" Ha! ha! ha!" laughed Joseph, as he drew him
back. " Hark'ee, Sir Peter, it is only a little
French milliner, a silly rogue that plagues me.

She has some character to lose, and on your coming she ran behind the screen."

"Ah, Joseph! Joseph! did I ever think that you——— But here's a closet that will do as well."

"Yes; go in there."

An amusing but very awkward scene followed. Now Lady Teazle peeped from behind the screen, and suggested that she might escape; and now Sir Peter thrust his head from the closet, and hoped that the little milliner would not blab. Joseph had his hands full to keep them from seeing each other, and was glad when Charles entered and relieved him of this difficulty.

It was not long, however, before the moral rogue found himself in a still deeper difficulty. For when, in accordance with his compact with Sir Peter, he taxed Charles with seeking to gain the affections of Lady Teazle, his brother answered that he had never dreamed of such a thing, and that he was surprised to hear this from him, whom he had always understood to be Lady Teazle's favorite.

Joseph sought to silence him, but Charles declared that he had seen them exchange significant glances, had found them together, and had——— Here Joseph, in despair of silencing his indiscreet brother in any other manner, was obliged to whisper to him that Sir Peter was in the closet and would hear all he said.

"In there!" cried Charles, gayly. "I'll have him out, then. Sir Peter, come forth." He threw open the closet door and dragged out the confused old spy. "What, my old guardian, turn inquisitor and take evidence incog? Oh, fie!"

"Give me your hand, Charles. I believe I have suspected you wrongfully. What I have heard has given me great satisfaction."

"Egad, then, it was lucky you didn't hear any more. Wasn't it, Joseph?"

"Ah! you would have retorted on him."

"Ay, ay, that was a joke."

"Yes, yes, I know his honor too well."

Joseph's troubles seemed fated to accumulate, for at this critical juncture the servant entered, and whispered to him that Lady Sneerwell was below and insisted on seeing him. She would not take no for an answer. He tried to get his visitors from the room, but they were bent on waiting there for his return, and he was obliged to leave them alone while he dismissed his lady caller on the plea of urgent business. Before leaving the room, however, he whispered to Sir Peter: "Not a word of the French milliner." "Not for the world," answered Sir Peter, and Joseph left the room with his uneasiness somewhat reduced.

He had not calculated sufficiently on the chapter of accidents. Hardly had he gone before Sir Peter began to praise his noble sentiments, and to express his belief that it would be greatly to the moral benefit of his dissolute brother if he would make him more of a companion. Charles answered that Joseph was too moral by half, and would, he supposed, as soon let a priest into his house as a woman.

"He is not such a saint either, in that respect," declared Sir Peter. "I have a great mind to tell him," he said to himself.

"Oh, hang him! he's a very anchorite! a young hermit."

"No, no," cried Sir Peter, with a laugh. "Egad, I'll tell him! Have you a mind to have a good laugh at Joseph?"

"I should like it of all things."

"Then, i' faith, I'll be even with him for discovering me! He had a girl with him when I called." Sir Peter's voice sank into a whisper.

"What! Joseph? You jest."

"Hush! a little French milliner. And the best of the jest is, she's in the room now."

"The devil she is!"

"Hush! I tell you," and Sir Peter pointed slily at the screen.

"Behind the screen? Let's unveil her!"

"No, no; he's coming; you sha'n't, indeed!"

"Yes, yes, we must have a peep at the little milliner."

"Not for the world! Joseph will never forgive me."

"I'll stand by you——"

Charles was not to be restrained in his mischievous humor, and just as Joseph opened the door to enter he threw down the screen, revealing

the lady behind it. The situation was truly a
startling one.

"Lady Teazle, by all that's wonderful!" cried
Charles.

"Lady Teazle, by all that's damnable!" groaned
Sir Peter.

As for Joseph, he stood in dumb silence, dis-
mayed beyond the power of speech.

"Sir Peter, this is one of the smartest French
milliners I ever saw," declared Charles. "Egad,
you all seem to have been diverting yourselves
at hide and seek. Your ladyship—Sir Peter—
morality—who will explain this secret? What!
all mute? Then I'll leave you to yourselves.
Brother, I'm sorry to find you have given that
worthy man grounds for so much uneasiness. Sir
Peter, there's nothing in the world so noble as a
man of sentiment," and with a gay laugh Charles
left the room.

What followed may be briefly told. Relieved of
his brother's presence, Joseph sought to clear
himself by a lying explanation of Lady Teazle's
presence. But unluckily for him that lady's sentiments and opinions had greatly changed since she
had been behind the screen, and she was by no
means disposed to second him. She declared that
all he had said was false, and that he had brought
her there for the purpose of seducing her. She
further said that the tender feeling for her which
her husband had expressed had so moved her
heart that she would devote her future life to

gratitude and affection. With these words she left the room.

"Notwithstanding all this, Sir Peter," began the discovered rogue, "heaven knows——"

"That you are a villain; and so I leave you to your conscience."

"You are too rash, Sir Peter; you shall hear me. The man who shuts out conviction by refusing to——"

"Oh! damn your sentiments!" cried Sir Peter, leaving the room in a rage. He had had enough of sentiment for the remainder of his life.

Joseph Surface's career of wordy morality and secret villany, indeed, was near its end, for events were ripening to expose him fully in his true character. It was not long after the scene we have described that Sir Oliver called upon him in his assumed character of Stanley, and begged for some aid in his distress. He found his nephew profuse in polite words, and full of seeming sorrow that his poverty would not let him aid the poor gentleman. Stanley professed surprise at this, saying that it was the common report that Sir Oliver had enriched his nephew; but Joseph declared that this was a mistake, and that the worthy but avaricious Indian merchant had only sent him a few trifling presents. Besides, he had lent such sums to his extravagant brother as quite to impoverish himself. In the end he politely bowed the visitor from the door, with obsequious expressions of esteem and good wishes, though he only succeeded in convincing Sir Oliver that he was a specious and selfish hypocrite.

Hardly had the pretended bankrupt left the house when word came to Joseph that his uncle, Sir Oliver, had arrived in London, and would soon call on him. In consternation, he sent in haste to recall Mr. Stanley, but it was too late. He had done himself irreparable mischief in that quarter. Should Mr. Stanley repeat to Sir Oliver what he had said, all his hopes of wealth from his rich uncle were at an end. And his plan to marry Sir Peter's wealthy ward Maria seemed equally hopeless after the late exposure. In fact, Charles Surface had made no secret of the amusing scene in his brother's library, and it was already in the hands of the scandal-mongers, who had magnified it into a serious duel, in which Sir Peter had been dangerously wounded.

The end was now near at hand. For while Joseph Surface was waiting in nervous anxiety for the promised visit of his uncle, a gentleman called whom he recognized as Mr. Stanley. He had desired to recall this person not long before, but now, when Sir Oliver was momentarily expected, his visit was most ill-timed, and the luckless schemer forgot his usual show of politeness in his haste to get rid of his unwelcome visitor.

As he was rudely pushing him out of the room, Charles Surface entered, and demanded to know what he was doing with his broker, little Premium. A scene of misunderstanding ensued, one brother insisting that the visitor was Mr. Stanley, who had come to borrow, and the other that it was Mr. Premium, who had come to lend. But both were satisfied that it would never do to have him seen by Sir Oliver, and Charles joined with Joseph in endeavoring to force him from the room, while he strenuously resisted.

In the midst of this scene the door was thrown open, and Sir Peter and Lady Teazle—who had become reconciled—entered, followed by Maria and Rowley. They looked in surprise on the scene before them.

"What, my old friend, Sir Oliver!" exclaimed Sir Peter. "Here are dutiful nephews, truly! assaulting their uncle at his first visit!"

"Indeed, Sir Oliver, it was well we came in to rescue you," said Lady Teazle.

"Truly it was," said Rowley, "for I perceive, Sir Oliver, the character of old Stanley was no protection to you."

"Nor of Premium, either," answered Sir Oliver. "The necessities of the former could not extort a shilling from that benevolent gentleman; and with the other I stood a chance of faring worse than my ancestors, and being knocked down without being bid for."

That the two brothers were in a state of the utmost consternation need not be said. The discovery had come upon them like a thunderbolt, and all hopes of inheriting a penny of their rich uncle's fortune seemed blown to the winds.

That this was the case in regard to Joseph was soon evident, for Sir Oliver lost no time in expressing his opinion of his meanness, to which Sir Peter and Lady Teazle added as strong sentiments concerning his treachery and hypocrisy.

"If they talk this way to Honesty, what will they say to me, by and by?" groaned Charles.

"Well, sir, in what way are you prepared to justify your prodigal behavior?" asked Sir Oliver, turning to him, after ending his remarks to his brother.

"In no way that I know of," answered Charles.

"What! Little Premium has been let too much into the secret?"

"Come, Sir Oliver," said Rowley. "I know you cannot speak of Charles's follies with anger."

"Nor with gravity either," answered Sir Oliver, with a laugh. "Do you know, Sir Peter, the rogue bargained with me for all his ancestors; sold me judges and generals by the foot, and maiden aunts as cheap as broken china."

"Why I did make a little free with the family canvas, Sir Oliver," acknowledged Charles. "Yet believe me sincere in saying that nothing could give me warmer satisfaction than to see you here before me, whatever opinion you may have formed of my follies."

"I believe you, Charles. Give me your hand; the ill-looking little fellow over the settee has made your peace."

"Then, sir, my gratitude to the original is still increased," answered Charles, gratefully.

But one more matter remained to be cleared up, the prodigal's relations to Maria. Though they loved each other truly, the young lady's ears had been so poisoned by calumnies concerning her lover, the invention of Joseph Surface, Lady Sneerwell, and Snake, that she declared she could have nothing to do with one who had played the traitor to another woman.

But, unluckily for the plot of the pair of conspirators, Rowley had got hold of Snake, and induced him to tell the truth. His evidence convicted the two arch rogues of villany, and overcame the objections of Maria, who now saw that the charges against her lover were all false, and gladly promised him her hand, on his sincere promise to reform.

And so ends the story of the two brothers, the hypocrite and the profligate. The former was cast off by his rich uncle, who advised him to marry his confederate, Lady Sneerwell. The latter was fully forgiven, his faults being those of youth and folly, not of meanness and treachery. He made no promise to reform, saying that he could not trust himself, but sincerly hoped that Maria would lead him into a better path. As for Sir Peter and Lady Teazle, their quarrels were at an end. She repented so bitterly her folly that she resolved thenceforth to return his love, and become a model of discretion.

THE RIVALS.

BY RICHARD BRINSLEY BUTLER SHERIDAN.

At the city of Bath, the famous English watering-place of the last century, had come together a number of persons of very peculiar character and habits. Two of the oddest among these were a young lady named Lydia Languish and her aunt Mrs. Malaprop. Miss Languish was notable for her highly romantic ideas. The books she read bore such titles as "The Delicate Distress," "The Tears of Sensibility," "The Sentimental Journey," and the like; a class of reading which could not but fill her with false ideas of life. Her wealth brought her many lovers, but of them all there was only one whom she thought worth a moment's consideration, and this from the fact that with him her course of true love ran far from smoothly. This favored lover was a young man named Beverley, an ensign in the British army, whose courtship Mrs. Malaprop so disapproved that she confined her niece to prevent her seeing him. But this was just the method to add fuel to Miss Lydia's fancy, since to her love's ideal lay in stolen interviews, an elopement, a clandestine marriage, and

184

all the other folly she had learned from sentimental novels.

"The dear delicious shifts I have been put to," she said to her confidante, "to gain half a minute's conversation with Beverley! How often have I stolen forth, in the coldest night in January, and found him in the garden, stuck like a dripping statue! There would he kneel to me in the snow, and sneeze and cough so pathetically, he shivering with cold and I with apprehension; and while the wild ... our hearts, how warmly would he press me ... play he came, and glow with mutual ardor! Ah, that was something like being in love.'

Had the romantic Lydia known the truth, her affection for her dear Beverley would have been sadly ... ... was desirous to be inetead of being an humble en... captain in the army, a son of Sir Anthony Absolute, and therefore a perfectly suitable connection. But knowing Miss Lydia's romantic fancy, and that she would not listen to any suitable courtship, he had assumed the name of Beverley, and wooed her under the guise of an ensign, the lowest grade in army rank. Miss Languish was heiress to a fortune of thirty thousand pounds, the greater part of which she would lose if she married before she came of age without her aunt's consent. But to commit this wild folly would be to her the very flower of love's romance, and she declared that she could never

all the other folly she had learned from sentimental novels.

"The dear delicious shifts I have been put to," she said to her confidante, "to gain half a minute's conversation with Beverley! How often have I stolen forth, in the coldest night in January, and found him in the garden, stuck like a dripping statue! There would he kneel to me in the snow, and sneeze and cough so pathetically; he shivering with cold and I with apprehension; and while the cold blast numbed our joints, how warmly would he press me to pity his flame, and glow with mutual ardor! Ah, that was something like being in love."

Had the romantic Lydia known the truth, her affection for her dear Beverley would have been sadly damped. The fact was that her lover was deceiving her. Instead of being an humble ensign, he was really a captain in the army, a son of Sir Anthony Absolute, and therefore a perfectly suitable connection. But knowing Miss Lydia's romantic fancy, and that she would not listen to any sensible courtship, he had assumed the name of Beverley, and wooed her under the guise of an ensign, the lowest grade in army rank. Miss Languish was heiress to a fortune of thirty thousand pounds, the greater part of which she would lose if she married before she came of age without her aunt's consent. But to commit this wild folly seemed to her the very flower of love's romance, and she declared that she could never

love the man who would ask for a day's delay
from base desire for her money.

At the time our story opens Lydia was in deep
trouble. She had never experienced the delight-
ful sensation of a quarrel with her lover, nor
would he give her the opportunity for one. This
was to her so out of the ordinary course of true
love, and so against all precedent in novels, that
she determined to invent a quarrel, since her lover
was so deliriously good-natured as not to yield
her a real one. With this laudable purpose, she
wrote a letter to herself, signing it "Your Friend
Unknown," in which she informed herself that
Beverley was paying his addresses to another
woman. This she showed to Beverley, and, pretending to be in a violent passion, charged him
with falsehood, and vowed she would never see
him again. Unfortunately for the success of this
little romance, her aunt just then discovered her
clandestine interviews and brought her to Bath,
where she confined her so closely to the house that
no opportunity was given for a reconciliation with
Beverley, and the poor silly maiden was in the
depths of despair, fearing that she had lost her
lover forever.

The aunt, Mrs. Malaprop, was as singular a character as the niece. She had a ridiculous habit of
using long words, which meant something very
different from what she intended, and gave a very
ludicrous turn to her conversation. As an example,
we may quote her views on female education.

"I would by no means wish a daughter of mine to be a progeny of learning," she said. "For instance, I would never let her meddle with Greek, or Hebrew, or algebra, or simony, or fluxions, or paradoxes, or such inflammatory branches of learning. But I would send her, at nine years old, to a boarding-school, to learn a little ingenuity and artifice. Then she should have a supercilious knowledge in accounts; and as she grew up I would have her instructed in geometry, that she might know something of the contagious countries; but, above all, she should be mistress of orthodoxy, that she might not misspell and mispronounce words so shamefully as girls usually do, and might reprehend the true meaning of what she is saying. This is what I would have a woman know; and I don't think there is a superstitious article in it."

Mrs. Malaprop, in her turn, was in love, the object of her ancient fancy being a fire-eating Irish baronet named Sir Lucius O'Trigger, whom she had met at a ball, and with whom she kept up a secret correspondence under the assumed name of Delia. Sir Lucius, under the belief that these romantic letters came from Miss Lydia Languish, with whom he fancied himself in love, was happy to reply in the same vein, and the air bore many a weight of love between these sentimental correspondents. The go-between of all these lovers was Lydia's maid, a shrewd minx, named Lucy, who pretended to be very simple, but was at once in the pay of Beverley, Sir Lucius, Lydia, Mrs. Malaprop, and Bob Acres, another of Miss Languish's lovers, a silly fellow whom she despised as much as she loved Beverley.

The above named are but a portion of the party who, as we have said, had assembled at Bath. One of the others was Captain Absolute, who had come hither under his own name, but with the hope of meeting Miss Lydia in his assumed character of Beverley. Another was his father, Sir Anthony, a high-tempered old gentleman, who knew nothing of his son's presence or of his secret love affair, and was likely to make trouble when he should find out what was going on. Two others were Julia, Lydia's confidential friend, and her lover, Mr. Faulkland, a young gentleman of such jealous affection that he made himself miserable through the constant fear that his love was not fully returned.

Sir Anthony Absolute had a special purpose in coming to Bath. He strongly desired to have his son marry Miss Languish, and wished to treat with Mrs. Malaprop to that end. This proposal he found quite agreeable to that lady, for she was afraid of some ill-result from her niece's romantic fancy, being especially troubled by the discovery of Lydia's penchant for Beverley.

"I will write for the boy directly," said Sir Anthony. "He knows not a syllable of this yet, though I have for some time had the proposal in my head."

Little did the good knight imagine that his graceless son was already secretly paying his addresses to the romantic young lady.

"We have never seen your son, Sir Anthony," said Mrs. Malaprop; "but I hope there will be no objection on his side."

"Objection! let him object if he dare!" cried Sir Anthony, angry at the very thought. "No, no, Mrs. Malaprop, Jack knows that the least demur puts me in a frenzy directly. My process was always very simple, in his younger days. It was 'Jack, do this'; if he demurred, I knocked him down, and if he grumbled at that, I sent him out of the room."

"Ay, the properest way, on my conscience," said Mrs. Malaprop. "Nothing is so conciliating to young people as severity. Well, Sir Anthony, I shall give Mr. Acres his discharge, and prepare Lydia to receive your son's invocations; and I hope you will represent her to the captain as an object not altogether illegible."

"Take my advice; keep a tight hand: if she rejects this proposal, clap her under lock and key; and if you were just to let the servants forget to bring her dinner for three or four days, you can't conceive how she'd come about."

"Well, at any rate, I shall be glad to get her from under my intuition."

Sir Anthony was not long in learning that his hopeful son had not waited to be summoned to Bath. He accidentally met Fag, the captain's servant, and on asking him what brought him there, was told that his master had come there to recruit, though he did not say whether for men, money, or health.

Fag hastened to warn his master of what had happened, that he might know what story to tell if he should meet his father. The young man's purpose in coming to Bath had been to put an end to the deception he had practised, and tell Lydia his real name and rank, but he felt that this must be done very cautiously; for he was convinced that though she would be glad to elope with him as Ensign Beverley, it was doubtful if she would accept him with her aunt's consent, a humdrum wedding, and the prospect of a fortune on his side. Marriage never took place in that way in her favorite novels, and she was likely to object decidedly to an unromantic matrimony.

Captain Beverley confided this critical state of his affairs to his friend Faulkland, whom he found in a fever of apprehension from a less reasonable cause. He was sorely troubled lest anxiety about his absence, or the inclemency of the weather, might have overcome his Julia's health.

"So, then, if you were convinced that Julia were well and in spirits, you would be entirely content?" asked Captain Absolute.

"I should be happy beyond measure," replied Faulkland.

"Then, to cure your anxiety at once, I may tell

you that Miss Melville is in perfect health, and is at this moment in Bath."

"Nay, Jack, don't trifle with me."

"She has arrived here with my father within this hour."

"My dear Jack! now, nothing on this earth can give me a moment's uneasiness."

The confident lover did not know himself, as was soon to be shown. For Bob Acres called at this point in their conversation, and, as this whimsical fellow lived near Miss Melville, Faulkland grew at once eager to learn from him how his lady love had borne his absence. After some introductory conversation, he remarked,—

"I have not seen Miss Melville yet; I hope she enjoyed full health and spirits in Devonshire."

"Never knew her better in my life, sir," answered Acres; "never better. Odds blushes and blooms! She has been as healthy as the German Spa."

"Indeed! I did hear she had been a little indisposed."

"False, false, sir; only said to vex you: quite the reverse, I assure you."

"There, Jack," said Faulkland, discontentedly, "and I had almost fretted myself ill. Isn't there something unkind in this violent, robust, unfeeling health?"

"Oh, to be sure, it was very unkind of her to be well in your absence," answered Jack.

"But, Mr. Acres," resumed the lover, "she

has been merry and gay, I suppose? Always in spirits, hey?"

"Merry, odds crickets! She has been the belle and spirit of the company wherever she has been. Then she is so accomplished,—so sweet a voice! Odds minions and crotchets, how she did chirrup at Mrs. Piano's concert!"

"Oh, the innate levity of woman!" groaned Faulkland. "Do you remember what songs Miss Melville sung?"

"Not I, indeed."

"Some pretty, melancholy, purling-stream airs I warrant," said Captain Absolute. "Did she sing, *When absent from my soul's delight*, or *Go, gentle gales?*"

"Oh no! nothing like that. Odds! now I recollect one of them,—*My heart's my own, my will is free*. And then her dancing——"

"Ah, yes! you were about to praise Miss Melville's manner of dancing a minuet, eh?" queried Faulkland.

"No, what I was going to speak of was her country-dancing. Odds swimming! she has such an air with her."

"There, there, I told you so!" cried Faulkland, in a fever of jealous uneasiness. "She thrives in my absence. Her whole feelings have been in opposition with mine. I have been anxious, silent, pensive, sedentary. She has been all health, spirit, laugh, song, dance. Fool, fool, that I am, to fix all my happiness on such a trifler! Tell me,

Jack, have I been the joy and spirit of the company?"

"No, indeed, you have not."

"Have I been full of wit and humor?"

"No, faith, to do you justice, you have been confoundedly stupid."

"Excuse me, Jack, I must leave. I own, I am somewhat flurried."

"Ha! ha! ha! poor fellow! Five minutes ago nothing on earth could give you a moment's uneasiness. But stay, Faulkland, and thank Mr. Acres for his good news."

"Confound his news!" exclaimed the angry lover, and he rushed from the room in a rage.

While Captain Absolute was thus amusing himself with the peevish love-folly of his friend, events were preparing which were destined to throw him into as deep a real trouble as the imaginary one into which Bob Acres's story had plunged Faulkland.

For hardly had his visitors left him than his father entered, full of his matrimonial scheme. He began in an indirect fashion, by telling his dear Jack that he considered the income allowed him as too small for a lad of his spirit, and that he had resolved to make him master of a large estate in a few weeks.

This auspicious opening filled the young man with joy; but this was turned to consternation when, in the midst of his thanks, his father informed him that a wife accompanied the gift.

"Why, what difference does that make?" demanded Sir Anthony, on his son's hasty exclamation of dissent. "Odds life, sir! if you have the estate you must take it with the live stock on it."

"If my happiness is to be the price," answered Jack, "I must beg leave to decline the purchase. Pray, sir, who is the lady?"

"What's that to you, sir?" cried his father, angrily. "Come, give me your promise to love and to marry her directly."

"You must excuse me, sir," was Jack's resolute reply, "if I tell you, once for all, that in this point I cannot obey you."

"Hark'ee, Jack," cried his father, with a flushed face, "I have heard you with patience; I have been cool,—quite cool; but take care,—you know I am compliance itself,—when I am not thwarted; no one more easily led,—when I have my own way,—but don't put me in a passion."

"Nay, sir, but hear me."

"I won't hear a word,—not a word! So give me your promise by a nod, you undutiful dog."

"What, sir, promise to link myself to some mass of ugliness!"

"Zounds, sirrah!" cried Sir Anthony, breaking into a violent rage, "the lady shall be as ugly as I choose; she shall have a hump on each shoulder; she shall be as crooked as the crescent; she shall have the skin of a mummy, and the beard of a Jew,—she shall be all this, sirrah!—yet I will make you ogle her all day, and sit up all night to write sonnets on her beauty."

Sir Anthony, in short, fretted himself into such a fury that he would not listen to a word that his son could say, and when Jack sought, in very mild language, to defend himself, broke out with,—

" So, you will fly out! Can't you be cool, like me? What the devil good can passion do? You rely on the mildness of my temper,—you do, you dog! You play upon the meekness of my disposition! But take care,—the patience of a saint may be overcome at last. Mark me, sirrah, I give you six hours and a half to consider of this; then, if you don't agree, without condition to do everything on earth that I choose, don't dare to breathe the same air or use the same light with me, but get an atmosphere and a sun of your own. I'll strip you of your commission! I'll disown you! I'll disinherit you! and, damn me, if I ever call you Jack again!"

And in a towering rage the old gentleman stamped from the room and down the stairs, fiercely thumping the balusters all the way, while at the bottom he gave Fag a blow on the head with his cane and kicked the cook's dog into the area, as some relief to his overcharged feelings.

That Captain Absolute found himself in an awkward dilemma need not be said. Fortunately, he was soon to be relieved from it, through the aid of his servant Fag, and Lucy, the bribe-taking maid. Lucy was abroad on an errand, from Mrs.

Malaprop, bearing to Sir Lucius a note which ran as follows, and which the worthy Irishman read with some perplexity:

"Sir,—There is often a sudden incentive impulse in love that has a greater induction than years of domestic combination; such was the commotion I felt at the first superfluous view of Sir Lucius O'Trigger. Female punctuation forbids me to say more; yet let me add, that it will give me joy infallible to find Sir Lucius worthy the last criterion of my affections. Delia."

"Upon my conscience, Lucy, your lady is a great mistress of language," exclaimed Sir Lucius. "Faith, she's the queen of the dictionary, for the devil a word dare refuse coming at her call, though one would think it was quite out of bearing."

After the Irish lover had departed, Lucy met Fag, whom she knew only as Beverley's servant, and told him, as a most valuable piece of news, that there was a worse rival than Bob Acres in the field, for Sir Anthony Absolute had proposed his son, Captain Absolute, as a suitor for Miss Languish's hand. These tidings, as may be imagined, failed to throw Fag into the consternation which Lucy had expected; and when, soon afterwards, he repeated the news to the downcast captain, it revived him as if all his veins had been filled with champagne. So his father wanted him to marry the very girl he was plotting to run away with! Here was information, indeed! The glad lover resolved to withdraw all his objections instantly, and to overcome his father's rage by a full consent to the projected marriage.

The opportunity to put his decision into effect soon came, for shortly after hearing Fag's welcome story he encountered his father. The old gentleman, who was still in a state of fury, vowed he would have nothing more to do with the rebel, and could hardly be brought to listen to his profession of penitence. But when the captain promised to yield to him in everything, the wind of his temper sank as suddenly as it had risen.

"Why, now you talk sense," he declared. "I never heard anything more reasonable in my life. Confound me! you shall be Jack again, and I will inform you who the lady really is. Nothing but your passion and violence prevented my telling you at first. What think you of Miss Lydia Languish?"

"Languish! What, the Languishes of Worcestershire?"

"Worcestershire! no, sir. Did you never meet Mrs. Malaprop and her niece, Miss Languish?"

"Malaprop! Languish! Stay, I think I do recollect something. Languish! Languish! She squints, don't she? A little red-haired girl?"

"Squints! A red-haired girl! Zounds! no."

"Then I must have forgot,—it can't be the same person."

"Jack, Jack, what think you of blooming, love-breathing seventeen?"

"As to that, sir, I am quite indifferent. If I can please you in the matter it is all I desire."

"Nay, but, Jack, such eyes! such blushing cheeks! such lovely smiling lips! such——"

"And which is to be mine, sir, the niece or the aunt?"

This exasperating question almost threw Sir Anthony into a rage again.

"Why, you unfeeling, insensible puppy!" he broke out, "I despise you! The aunt, indeed! Odds life! when I ran away with your mother I would not have touched anything old or ugly to gain an empire."

"Not to please your father, sir?"

"To please my father! zounds! not to please —— Oh, my father—odds so!—yes, yes; if my father indeed had desired,—that's quite another matter. But he wasn't the indulgent father that I am, Jack."

"I dare say, not, sir."

Jack carried his penitential professions somewhat too far, as it proved, for his father began to suspect him of hypocrisy, and at length broke out with,—

"Come along with me; you shall visit the lady directly; and I'll never forgive you if you don't come back stark mad with rapture and impatience. If you don't, egad, I'll marry the girl myself!"

"In that case, sir, I suppose you would have me marry the aunt. Or if you should change your mind, and take the old lady,—it is all the same to me,—I'll marry the niece."

This was more than Sir Anthony could stand. He flung himself angrily from the room, leaving Jack with a sly smile on the leeward side of his face. But in a few minutes the old gentleman returned in a more peaceable temper, and with a note of introduction to Mrs. Malaprop, which he commanded his son to deliver immediately. This Jack dutifully obeyed, though not without many misgivings, for he feared the effect on Lydia's romantic fancy when she should discover that Beverley and Captain Absolute were one and the same.

Jack's interview with Mrs. Malaprop was not without its elements of awkwardness, for she informed him that the girl had fixed her affections on a beggarly ensign, and that, in spite of her positive "conjunctions," the fellow "persisted from" correspondence with her. She had just "interceded" another letter from him, she declared, which had given her the "hydrostatics" to such a degree.

Jack was not surprised at her "hydrostatics" on reading the letter, for it spoke of Mrs. Malaprop as an "old weather-beaten she-dragon," with other equally uncomplimentary epithets. Should the old lady discover that he had written this letter himself his hopes might be seriously interfered with, and he felt it necessary to play his cards with all the skill at his command.

It would be a happy idea, he told her, since the girl was so infatuated with Beverley, to let them plan an elopement; he would come in just at the nick of time, lay the fellow by the heels, and fairly contrive to carry her off in his stead. This scheme seemed to the good lady an excellent one, and she agreed to it on the spot. Then, laughing heartily at the idea of the lovers eluding her vigilance, she went out to send Lydia to her suitor.

Lydia's coming was a very unwilling one. She wanted nothing to do with this new suitor, and did not see why she should be pestered with hateful addresses. What, therefore, was her joyful surprise, when she at length entered the room, to recognize in the unwelcome visitor her dear Beverley! The lover, however, had his presence to explain, and did so by telling her that he had passed himself off upon Mrs. Malaprop as Captain Absolute, a piece of invented information which filled the girl with delight.

Unluckily, in the midst of their transports of affection, Mrs. Malaprop made her appearance at the door, where she overheard a part of their conversation. All would have been now in danger, but that she misunderstood the meaning of their words, and revealed her presence before they were too deeply committed.

"Let her choice be Captain Absolute," said Lydia, "but Beverley is mine."

"Oh, you vixen! I have overheard you," cried

Mrs. Malaprop, coming forward. "My dear captain, I know not how to apologize for her shocking rudeness."

The lover, who had started violently on hearing the good lady's voice, perceived by her words that his secret was still safe, and quietly remarked,—

"I have hopes, madam, that time will bring the young lady——"

"Oh, there's nothing to be hoped for from her," interrupted Mrs. Malaprop, pettishly. "She's as headstrong as an allegory on the banks of the Nile."

"Nay, pray, Mrs. Malaprop, don't stop the young lady's speech. She is very welcome to profess love for Beverley,—it does not hurt me in the least, I assure you."

"You are too amiably patient, captain. Come with me, miss; but take a graceful leave of the gentleman."

"May every blessing wait on my Beverley," began Lydia, "my loved Bev——"

"Hussy! come along—come along," exclaimed the angry aunt, hurrying her out, the captain lovingly kissing his hand to her as she disappeared.

Meanwhile new complications were arising for the gallant captain, as a consequence of his double character. Before long, indeed, he had two duels on his hand, one as Beverley and the other as Captain Absolute.

Bob Acres, who had followed Lydia to Bath to continue his suit, had been summarily dismissed, and fancied that he was thrown aside in favor of Beverley, who he had heard was in Bath. He complained of this affront to Sir Lucius O'Trigger, who assured him that he had been very shabbily treated, and that his wounded honor could only be healed by shedding the blood of his rival.

"But he has given me no provocation," declared Bob. "Faith, I never saw the man in my life."

"That's no argument at all," answered Sir Lucius. "He has the less right, then, to take the liberty to fall in love with the same woman as yourself."

"Gad, that's true!" exclaimed Bob, filled with sudden valor. "I grow full of anger, Sir Lucius. I fire apace. Odds hilts and blades, I find a man may have a deal of valor in him, and not know it! But couldn't I contrive to have a little right on my side?"

"What the devil signifies *right*, when your *honor* is concerned? Do you think Achilles, or my little Alexander the Great, ever inquired where the right lay?"

"Odds flints, paws, and triggers! I'll challenge him directly."

"Ah, my little friend, if I had Blunderbuss Hall here, I could show you a glorious range of ancestry in the O'Trigger line,—every one of whom had killed his man!"

"I have had ancestors, too!" cried Bob, "every man of 'em colonel or captain in the militia. Odds balls and barrels! Say no more,—I'm braced for it. The thunder of your words has soured the milk of human kindness in my breast. 'Zounds!' as the man in the play says, 'I could do such deeds——'"

"Come, come, there must be no passion in the case. These things should always be done civilly."

"I must be in a passion, Sir Lucius,—I must be in a rage. Dear Sir Lucius, let me be in a rage, if you love me. Come, here's pen and paper. I would the ink were red. How shall I begin?"

"Decently, and like a Christian. Begin 'Sir——'"

"That's too civil by half."

"'To prevent the confusion that might arise from our both addressing the same lady, I shall expect the honor of your company——'"

"Zounds!" exclaimed Bob; "I'm not asking him to dinner."

"'To settle our pretensions——'"

"Well?"

"Let me see,—'in King's Mead-fields.'"

"So that's done."

"Now, I'll leave you to fix your own time," said Sir Lucius. "Take my advice and decide it this evening if you can; then let the worst come of it, 'twill be off your mind to-morrow."

"Very true."

"I would do myself the honor to carry your

message; but, to tell you a secret, I believe I shall have just such another affair on my own hands. There is a gay captain here who put a jest on me lately, at the expense of my country, and I only want to fall in with the gentleman to call him out."

"By my valor, I should like to see you fight first! Odds life! I should like to see you kill him, if it was only to get a little lesson."

"I shall be very proud of instructing you. But for the present am obliged to bid you good day," and the gallant Sir Lucius took himself off, leaving Bob to the difficult task of keeping alive his courage, and to the necessary duty of getting some friend to deliver his challenge. For this warlike task he settled on Captain Absolute.

"You know something of this fellow," declared Bob, on meeting the captain. "I want you to find him out for me, and give him this mortal defiance."

"Trust me to see that he gets it," replied Jack, managing to conceal his laughter at this idea of conveying a challenge to himself.

"You couldn't be my second, could you, Jack?"

"Why no, Bob; there are reasons——"

"Well, well, I must ask Sir Lucius. But, Jack, if Beverley should ask you what kind of a man your friend Acres is, do tell him I am a devil of a fellow. Will you, Jack?"

"To be sure I shall. I'll say you are a determined dog, hey, Bob!"

"Ay, do. Tell him I generally kill a man a week, will you, Jack?"

"I will. I'll say you are called in the country, Fighting Bob."

"True, true; and, Jack, you may add that you never saw me in such a rage before,—a devouring rage."

"I will, I will."

"Egad, I hope that may frighten him so that he won't come. It is all to prevent mischief, Jack. I don't want to take his life, if I can clear my honor."

This challenge was soon followed by the threatened one from Sir Lucius O'Trigger, who was not the man to let an insult to his native island pass unrevenged. Luckily for the Irishman's purpose, he met with Jack when he was in a very ill-humor from something which had just happened, and was more ready to fight than to eat. He accepted the challenge of Sir Lucius, therefore, with few words, and made the hour and the place the same that had been appointed for Bob Acres's fight with Beverley.

It is necessary now to go back and relate the cause of Jack's ill-humor. He had abundant reason to be ruffled in temper, for his love affair had got into a very awkward snarl. In fact, Sir Anthony had insisted on accompanying him on a visit to Mrs. Malaprop and Lydia, and there, in spite of all that the cunning lover could do to prevent an exposure, the truth of his deception came out. Lydia, in short, had refused so strongly to accept him as Captain Absolute, and so earnestly insisted that he was her Beverley, that he was left no escape but to confess the truth, and throw himself on her mercy.

His confession was differently received by the three parties present. Lydia fell into a tearful pet at the idea that there would be no elopement after all. Mrs. Malaprop recalled, with angry countenance, Beverley's epithet of "a weatherbeaten she-dragon." As for Sir Anthony, he broke out heartily with,—

"Upon my soul, Jack, you are a very impudent fellow! You have made a fool of your father, you dog! So this was your 'penitence,' your 'duty and obedience'! What, 'the Languishes of Worcestershire,' hey? What, 'she squints, don't she?—a little red-haired girl'! hey? Why, you hypocritical young rascal! I wonder you ain't ashamed to hold up your head! Well, well, I am glad, at any rate, you are not the dull, insensible varlet you pretended to be."

But Jack did not find Miss Lydia so forgiving as his father and her aunt proved to be. Left alone with the deceived young lady, he found her sullen and freezing. The idea that she was expected to marry with the full consent of her friends, a license, settlements, all the every-day commonplaces of matrimony, so overturned her ideals that she repulsed him in peevish discontent, and in the end broke into a passion and flung his picture at him, vowing that she never wished to see his treacherous face again. The interview ended in a hot quarrel, in which Lydia declared that she renounced the counterfeit Beverley forever, and which left her lover in the humor to cut the throats of ten fighting Irishmen.

But we must for the moment return to Faulkland, whose love affair we left in a very unsatisfactory condition. He was not long in making it still more unsatisfactory; in an interview with Julia, he blamed her bitterly for her high spirits in Devonshire, and was generally so unreasonable as to drive her from the room in tears. In a second interview he tried a plan he had devised to test her love; professing to have committed an act that would oblige him to fly in haste from England, and calling on her for sympathy and love. Julia, filled with grief and alarm, at once consented to fly with him; upon which Faulkland, filled with joy at this proof of her love, acknowledged that he had deceived her, and begged her pardon for thus testing her love. His confession had a different effect than he anticipated. The poor woman felt that her feelings had been outraged, and told him that his test of love was an insult, that she could never be happy with such an exacting lover, and that she would never be his,—he had broken the last link of her affection. With these words she resolutely retired, leaving Faulkland in as awkward a situation and as depressed a mood as was Captain Absolute, though from a very different cause.

Julia, on leaving her lover, sought her friend and confidante Lydia, her heart full of pain, her eyes still wet with tears. She found her romantic friend plunged into as great a trouble as herself. To think that her dear Beverley should turn out to be this prosily eligible Captain Absolute, and that dull common sense was to preside over her matrimonial affair!

"Is it not provoking," she exclaimed, "when I thought we were coming to the prettiest distress imaginable, to find myself made a mere Smithfield bargain of at last? I had projected one of the most sentimental elopements! so becoming a disguise! so amiable a ladder of ropes! Conscious moon—four horses—Scotch parson—with such surprise to Mrs. Malaprop—and such paragraphs in the newspaper! Oh, I shall die with disappointment!"

"I don't wonder at it," answered Julia.

"Now,—sad reverse!—what have I to expect, but, after a deal of flimsy preparation with a bishop's license, and my aunt's blessing, to go simpering up to the altar; or perhaps be cried three times in a country church, and have an unmannerly fat clerk ask the consent of every butcher in the parish to join John Absolute and Lydia Languish, spinster? Oh, that I should live to hear myself called spinster!"

"Melancholy, indeed!" sympathized Julia, while Lydia walked the floor in a pet of temper.

Luckily for her, her love affair was not to be too dismally commonplace. Her lover was about to fight a duel for the privilege of her hand, and tidings of this alarming event were even now on their way to her.

Bob Acres had told the story of his challenge to his servant David, who was, if possible, a more arrant coward than himself; and David, who could not be made to see how his master would be the better off to have his honor alive and himself dead, lost no time in giving the alarm.

Failing to find Sir Anthony, he ran in haste to Mrs. Malaprop's, and told his tale of battles and bloodshed to that lady and to Tag, the captain's servant, whom he found there. Mrs. Malaprop, alarmed at the news, burst, in her turn, into the room where Julia and Lydia were exchanging confidences, and cried out,—

"So! so! here's fine work! here's fine suicide, paracide, and simulation going on in the fields! and Sir Anthony not to be found to prevent the antistrophe!"

"For heaven's sake, madam, what is the meaning of this?" asked Julia.

"Dear aunt, do tell us what is the matter?" demanded Lydia.

"Why, murder's the matter! slaughter's the matter! killing's the matter! But this gentleman can tell you the perpendiculars."

"Who, sir,—who are engaged in this?" asked Lydia.

"Faith, ma'am," answered Tag, "one is a young gentleman whom I should be sorry anything was to happen to,—a very pretty behaved gentleman."

"But who—who—who?" cried Lydia, impatiently.

"My master, ma'am."

"Heavens! What, Captain Absolute?"

"Who is there beside Captain Absolute?" demanded Julia.

"My poor master," said David. "My master, Mr. Acres. Then comes Squire Faulkland."

"Oh, madam," exclaimed Julia, "let us instantly endeavor to prevent mischief!"

"No, no," said Mrs. Malaprop. "That would be very inelegant in us; we should only participate things."

"Ah, do save a few lives!" pleaded David. "They are desperately given, believe me. Above all, there is that blood-thirsty Philistine, Sir Lucius O'Trigger."

"Sir Lucius O'Trigger!" exclaimed Mrs. Malaprop. "Oh, mercy! have they drawn poor, little, dear Sir Lucius into the scrape? Why, how you stand, girl! You have no more feeling than one of the Derbyshire petrifactions."

"What are we to do?" asked Lydia.

"Why, fly with the utmost felicity, to prevent mischief. Here, friend, can you show us the place?"

"If you please, ma'am, I will conduct you," said Tag. "David, do you look for Sir Anthony."

"Come, girls, this gentleman will exhort us," said Mrs. Malaprop. "Come, sir, you're our envoy,—lead the way, and we'll precede."

Tag hastened to obey orders, and in a few minutes the frightened ladies were on their way to the field of battle.

About the same time Sir Anthony met his son in the streets on his way to the place of combat. Jack was armed for the duel, and endeavored to conceal his sword under his cloak, but his father discovered it, and demanded to know what he was up to now.

"Sir, I'll explain," answered Jack. "You know, sir, Lydia is romantic, devilish romantic, and very absurd. Now I intend, if she refuses to forgive me, to unsheathe this sword and swear to fall upon its point and die at her feet."

"Fall upon a fiddlestick's end!" growled Sir Anthony. "Why, it is the very thing that would please her. Get along, you fool!"

This Jack was very ready to do. But hardly had he disappeared before David appeared, white with terror, and revealed the true secret of the sword. Swearing like a trooper at the trick of his worthy son, Sir Anthony bade David lead him to the field,—whither the three ladies were just then hurrying at all speed.

Of the various combatants, Sir Lucius and Bob

Acres were the first to reach the field of battle. They were provided with pistols.

"Tell me, Mr. Acres," said Sir Lucius, "in case of an accident, is there any little commission I could execute for you?"

"I—I don't understand," declared Bob, trembling like a leaf.

"Why, there's no being shot at without a little risk. Suppose now an unlucky bullet should carry a quietus with it, would you choose to be pickled and sent home? Or would it be the same to you to lie here in the Abbey? I'm told there is very snug lying in the Abbey."

"Pickled! Snug lying in the Abbey! Don't talk so, Sir Lucius."

"But there's nothing like being prepared. Pray, now, how will you receive the gentleman's fire?"

"Odd! I'll make myself small enough; I'll stand edgeways."

"You're quite out there, Mr. Acres. If the bullet misses a vital part of your right side, it will be very hard if it don't succeed on the left. But if you present your full front, a ball or two may pass clean through your body and never do any harm at all."

"A ball or two clean through me!" cried Bob, shaking with terror.

"And then it's the genteelist attitude."

"Look you, Sir Lucius; I'd as lieve be shot in an awkward posture as a genteel one; so, by my valor, I will stand edgeways."

"Sure, they don't mean to disappoint us?" said Sir Lucius, looking at his watch. "No, faith, I think I see them coming. Who are those yonder getting over the stile?"

"Well,—let them come,—hey, Sir Lucius! we-we-we-we—won't run."

"Run?"

"No—I say—we won't run."

"What the devil's the matter with you?" exclaimed the bold second, looking angrily at his trembling principal.

"Nothing—nothing, my dear friend,—but I—I—I don't feel quite so bold, somehow, as I did."

"Well, here they're coming."

"Sir Lucius, if I wasn't with you, I should almost think I was afraid. If my valor should leave me,—valor will come and go."

"Then, pray, keep it fast while you have it."

"Sir Lucius, I doubt it is going,—yes, my valor is certainly going,—it is sneaking off,—I feel it oozing out, as it were, at the palms of my hands."

"Your honor, sir,—your honor. Here they are."

Fortunately for Bob's valor, no Beverley appeared. But after some conversation Captain Absolute acknowledged that he was Beverley, and as such was quite willing to give Mr. Acres satisfaction. But the courageous Bob quite declined to quarrel with his dear friend Jack Absolute.

"Upon my conscience, Mr. Acres," declared Sir Lucius, "your valor has oozed away with a vengeance."

"Not in the least," retorted Bob. "I'll be your second with all my heart, and if you should get a quietus, I'll get you snug lying in the Abbey here; or pickle you and send you over to Blunderbuss Hall, or anything of the kind, with the greatest pleasure."

"Sir Lucius, you can't have a better second than my friend Acres," said Captain Absolute. "He is a most determined dog,—called in the country, Fighting Bob. He generally kills a man a week. Don't you, Bob?"

"Ay,—at home," answered Bob.

One duel still remained,—that between Sir Lucius and Captain Absolute; but before it could be fought the duellists were interrupted by Sir Anthony and the three ladies, one of them in a rage, the others overcome with terror.

"Put up, Jack, put up, or I shall be in a frenzy!" exclaimed Sir Anthony. "How came you in a duel, sir?"

"Faith, sir, that gentleman can tell you better than I," answered his son. "He called me out, without explaining his reasons."

"Gad, sir, how came you to call my son out without explaining your reasons?"

"Your son, sir, insulted me in a manner which my honor could not brook," replied Sir Lucius.

"Zounds, Jack, how durst you insult the gentleman in a manner which his honor could not brook?"

"Come, come, let's have no honor before ladies,"

exclaimed Mrs. Malaprop. "Captain Absolute, how could you intimidate us so? Here's Lydia has been terrified to death for you."

"For fear I should be killed, or escape, ma'am?"

"Nay, no delusions to the past. Lydia is convinced. Speak, child."

There followed a series of explanations, which proved quite to the satisfaction of all parties concerned except Sir Lucius; who, on discovering that his Delia was not the fair Julia, but her aunt, Mrs. Malaprop, felt himself quickly cured of his romantic passion.

As for Lydia, her fright at the danger of her lover, and satisfaction that he was ready to fight a duel on her account, made her ready to forgive the counterfeit Beverley, and accept him without an elopement, while Julia proved as kind to her exacting lover. All the difficulties which had surrounded the two pairs of lovers were, therefore, happily removed, Bob Acres and Sir Lucius gallantly promising to dance at their weddings, while happiness, in the form of Hymen, spread its wings over the reconciled Rivals.

END OF VOL. II.